SWEET VALLEY HIGH

FAMILY SECRETS

Written by
Kate William

Created by
FRANCINE PASCAL

BANTAM BOOKS
TORONTO • NEW YORK • LONDON • SYDNEY • AUCKLAND

RL 6, IL age 12 and up

FAMILY SECRETS
A Bantam Book / May 1988

*Sweet Valley High® and Sweet Valley Twins are trademarks
of Francine Pascal.*

Conceived by Francine Pascal

*Produced by Daniel Weiss Associates, Inc.
27 West 20 Street
New York, NY 10011*

Cover art by James Mathewuse.

ISBN 0-553-27176-8

Published simultaneously in the United States and Canada

*Bantam Books are published by Bantam Books, a division of Bantam Doubleday
Dell Publishing Group, Inc. Its trademark, consisting of the words "Bantam
Books" and the portrayal of a rooster, is Registered in U.S. Patent and Trademark
Office and in other countries. Marca Registrada. Bantam Books, 666 Fifth Avenue,
New York, New York 10103.*

PRINTED IN THE UNITED STATES OF AMERICA

O   0 9 8 7 6 5 4 3 2 1

FAMILY
SECRETS

FAMILY SECRETS

As Kelly leaned over the rail, waiting for Kirk to return, she remembered every minute she had spent with him that night. The more she thought about him, the more she liked him; he was even honest enough to admit he wanted to talk to an old friend without making a big deal about it. She smiled as she thought about him. Yes, he was special, she decided happily.

After several minutes, though, Kelly began to feel a twinge of impatience. She craned her neck to see if she could see him down the beach. She drummed her fingers on the railing. Catching up with an old friend was fine, but Kelly wondered what was taking him so long.

She finally sat down in a deck chair and crossed her legs restlessly. Just then, Kirk hurried toward her.

"Sorry," he said quickly. "My friend started in with this real hard luck story, and I couldn't get back here as quickly as I wanted to. All I kept thinking was how much I wished it were you I was talking to instead of her."

Kelly's irritation vanished instantly as she gazed into his intense blue eyes. "That's OK," she replied, "I understand."

"I knew you would." He held out his hand and gave her one of his irresistible, sexy smiles. "Now how about another dance?" he suggested, pulling her to her feet.

As though hypnotized, Kelly nodded and allowed him to lead her back to the dance floor.

One

"Liz! Wake up!"

Elizabeth Wakefield rolled over and grumbled sleepily. She was still lingering over an especially good dream. She and her boyfriend, Jeffrey French, were walking hand in hand along the beach, the foamy surf washing up over their ankles as the sun dropped in a golden glow into the rolling blue Pacific.

Without warning, her pillow was yanked out from under her and thumped on her head.

"Jessica!" she cried, pushing herself up and grabbing the pillow with one hand. "Are you trying to give me a concussion?" As Elizabeth opened her eyes and scrambled to a sitting position in her bed, her twin sister crossed to the window and snapped up the shade. A blaze of sunshine poured into the cozy room.

"Nope," Jessica replied airily as she opened

the window. Her blue-green eyes twinkled as she added, "I was sick of hearing you snore, that's all."

Elizabeth giggled and stretched her arms above her head. "Mmm. It looks like it's going to be a nice— Jessica, I just remembered!" Her eyes wide, she sat up straight.

Jessica dropped down on the end of Elizabeth's bed. "That's right, big sister. Today's the day. Kelly's coming."

Elizabeth drew her knees up to her chin and hugged her arms around her legs. One of their cousins, Kelly Bates, was arriving that afternoon from Tucson to stay with them for a while. As an only child, Kelly was having a rough time dealing with the fact that her mother was planning on remarrying a doctor with two children of his own. And on top of that, she had some other serious conflicts with her mother. Kelly was going to stay with the Wakefields until the tensions eased up a bit between her and her mother.

"I wonder if she still looks like us," Elizabeth mused. "Think so?"

Jessica tossed her hair over her shoulders. "I hope not. Two of us is too much for most people already!"

"That's true," Elizabeth agreed with a giggle.

Elizabeth and Jessica were identical twins. From their golden hair, dimpled left cheeks,

2

and dazzling smiles to their five-foot-six-inch figures and healthy California tans, the sixteen-year-old Wakefield twins were mirror images of each other.

But the similarities stopped when it came to their personalities. Elizabeth was steady, thoughtful, and practical. She liked books and heart-to-heart talks with her best friend, Enid Rollins, and her steady boyfriend, Jeffrey French. Writing a weekly column for the Sweet Valley High *Oracle* was her way of reaching for her dream—to be an author. Most of her experiences ended up in her personal journal, and her most adventurous experiences usually involved her twin.

That was because Jessica was daring, headstrong, and often more than a little reckless. Jessica liked to act first, then think—if she thought at all! Often Elizabeth ended up trying to restore order after Hurricane Jessica had swept through. As the older twin by four minutes, Elizabeth usually felt like the "big sister" in more ways than one.

"Two of us is definitely enough," Elizabeth continued with a wry grin. "Kelly did look a lot like us when we were little, though, that's for sure."

"Well, I can't wait to see her." Jessica flopped over onto her back on the bed and stared at the ceiling for a moment. Then she turned her head and gave Elizabeth a stern look. "Aren't you ever going to get up?" she demanded impatiently.

"OK! OK!" Chuckling, Elizabeth pushed back the covers and got out of bed. "This is obviously one Saturday morning I don't get to sleep late."

When the twins walked into the sunny, Spanish-tiled kitchen a few minutes later, their parents were already at the table with the newspaper and steaming mugs of coffee.

"Morning, girls," Alice Wakefield said with a happy smile. Her blue eyes sparkled as she added, "Everything all set for Kelly?" Kelly's mother was one of Mrs. Wakefield's sisters, and the twins knew their mother was thrilled at having her niece for an extended visit.

Jessica nodded through a long sip of fresh orange juice. "Yup. My room's cleaner than it's been in about five years."

"Will wonders never cease," Elizabeth commented dryly as she poured herself some cereal. Jessica's room, known in the family as "The Hershey Bar" since the time Jessica had painted the walls dark brown, usually looked like a disaster area. But the girls had decided that Kelly would share Jessica's room for the first half of her stay, then move in with Elizabeth. So Jessica had been tidying up for several days.

Tall, dark-haired Ned Wakefield lowered his

section of the paper and gave Jessica a look of surprise. "I think I should get the camera and take a picture—as evidence of a completely new phenomenon."

"Hardy-har-har," Jessica retorted sarcastically. Then she peered up at her father and grinned. "Is Steve going with us to the airport?"

"He can't make it," Mr. Wakefield replied, blowing gently on his coffee. "He has to go up to Puget Sound for a research project. But he'll try to come as soon as he can." The twins' older brother, Steven, was a freshman at a state university, but he often managed to get home to visit.

Elizabeth sat down at the table and propped her chin up on her hands. "It's been so long since we've seen Kelly. Ever since Aunt Laura left Uncle Greg and moved to Tucson." She frowned. "How long ago was it—eight years?"

"Mmm," Mrs. Wakefield agreed.

"You know," Jessica said, peeling a banana, "I never did understand why she left Sweet Valley like that."

Mrs. Wakefield's mouth tightened. "Your Aunt Laura had every reason to leave Greg," she said tersely.

Across the table Elizabeth and Jessica exchanged a meaningful look. They had heard enough about their uncle to know he wasn't exactly the ideal husband. He had always been

5

handsome and notoriously charming. But he had also cheated on his wife and then sworn never to do it again—again and again. He had a terrible temper and always apologized extravagantly for losing it. Their aunt had put up with a lot. But finally one night she had packed up eight-year-old Kelly, taken a plane for Tuscon, and later filed for divorce. No one ever talked about the incident, but Elizabeth suspected that something terrible must have happened.

"But, girls," Mrs. Wakefield continued as she looked at each of them in turn, her blue eyes clouded with worry, "Aunt Laura has made it a policy not to prejudice Kelly against her father. She doesn't believe in telling Kelly any of the bad memories she has, because she thinks Kelly should have good feelings about him. And she made me promise that we would respect that." She drew in a deep breath and let it out slowly. She was obviously unhappy about making that promise. "So as long as Kelly is here, no negative comments about her father. All right?"

"Sure, Mom," Elizabeth said solemnly. Jessica nodded.

For a moment Mrs. Wakefield stared moodily into her coffee cup. Then she managed a bright smile. "OK, who wants eggs?"

Kelly Bates pressed her forehead against the

small square window, straining for her first look at Southern California in eight years. In just a few minutes she would finally be home. Tucson had never felt right to her, and she blamed her mother for making them stay there. But things were going to change, Kelly vowed silently.

Suddenly her eyes filled with tears, and she blinked them back with impatience. As the plane descended swiftly, Kelly sat back and gripped the armrests, bracing herself.

"Is this your first flight?" the woman next to her asked with a kind smile.

Kelly laughed and shook her head. "No. I'm just so excited about seeing my cousins, that's all. I haven't seen them in years."

The plane bumped gently onto the ground, and the engines roared as the pilot slowed down the plane. In moments they were taxiing toward the terminal building. Her heart pounding, Kelly began gathering her things together. She couldn't wait to see everyone: Aunt Alice, Uncle Ned, the twins, and Steven.

As soon as the Fasten-Seat-Belt sign blinked off, she edged out into the aisle. The line of passengers shuffled toward the front of the plane and into the portable corridor attached to the main terminal. Once inside the terminal, she hurried to the area behind the security check, where people waited for arriving planes.

Kelly could feel the huge grin on her face as

she walked toward the spot where a crowd had gathered. Suddenly she spotted the twins, and the next moment she felt herself enveloped in a hug.

"Kelly!" Elizabeth and Jessica shrieked simultaneously.

"Hi," she gasped, hugging back instinctively. "Hi!"

Elizabeth and Jessica stepped back for a moment, and Kelly was immediately hugged again by her Aunt Alice. "Kelly. It's so good to have you here, sweetheart."

When she was able to catch her breath, Kelly took a good look at the Wakefields. Everyone looked just as she remembered, only older. She turned to the twins. "I know I can tell you apart," she said eagerly. They grinned back at her with excitement. "You're Liz, and you're Jess."

"No, wrong way." Elizabeth laughed. She sent Jessica a lopsided grin. "Jessica is the one without a wristwatch. That's the acid test. She never cares what time it is."

"But it won't take long to figure out which of us is which," Jessica assured her promptly. "After all, I'm the prettier one," she joked. "Don't worry about it."

Kelly grinned. She took a deep breath and looked from the twins to her aunt and uncle. "Well, here I am."

8

Ned Wakefield chuckled. "You sure are. Why don't you give me your baggage claim stubs, and you all can take a minute to get reacquainted."

With a grateful nod Kelly handed over her claim checks. She could already tell that her uncle must be a perfect father—just as she knew her own father would have been if her mother had only given him half a chance. Ned Wakefield gave her a wink and strode toward the baggage claim area.

"We can't wait for everyone to meet you!" Jessica exclaimed, taking Kelly by the arm.

Elizabeth took Kelly's other arm and grinned. "And they're really going to be surprised, too. You still do look a *lot* like us."

"There *is* a very strong family resemblance," Mrs. Wakefield commented.

Kelly bit her lower lip as she looked from the twins to her aunt and back again. "I can't believe I'm here," she said.

Elizabeth met her eyes with a soft smile and a look of complete understanding that made Kelly feel good. When they were children, she had shared more interests with Elizabeth than with Jessica. She and Elizabeth had both loved *Alice's Adventures in Wonderland*, and they used to act out the Mad Hatter's tea party and the crazy croquet game. And she knew, from letters, that Elizabeth wrote for the school newspaper and composed poetry, too, which Kelly had been doing for the last two years.

"Hey, here's Dad," Jessica announced. "That was fast."

When Mr. Wakefield joined them, he set Kelly's two big suitcases down with a gasp. "I can see you inherited the same wardrobe genes Jessica got," he teased. "Have you got bricks in here or something?"

"I guess I went kind of overboard," Kelly admitted, smiling. "But I wasn't sure what to bring."

"Don't worry—our clothes are your clothes," Elizabeth said with a wink. "My clothes are already Jessica's clothes anyway. At least they're mostly in her room."

"That's not true, and you know it," Jessica said in a mock injured tone. She gave the group an impatient look. "Well? Let's get out of here!"

"Yes, ma'am," Mr. Wakefield replied with a salute. He added to Kelly behind one hand, "She's so bossy, we're all terrified of her."

Giggling, Kelly followed along as they trooped out to the parking lot and piled into the Wakefields' car. Soon they were driving toward Sweet Valley. On both sides of Kelly, Elizabeth and Jessica kept up a constant stream of chatter.

"You'll have to officially register at school," Elizabeth told her. "But Mr. Cooper, the principal, already knows you'll be staying for a cou-

10

ple of months, and he'll probably give you the official welcome-to-Sweet-Valley-High speech. It's pretty boring, but his intentions are good."

"His intentions are boring," Jessica corrected. "But as the real welcome to Sweet Valley, we have a much better surprise for you," she went on, her eyes sparkling with excitement.

Kelly felt her own eyes widen with anticipation. "What?" She looked from Jessica to Elizabeth and back again.

Putting one hand on Kelly's arm, Elizabeth explained. "Jessica always has to make such a drama out of everything. It's just that there's a friend of ours we think you'd really like to meet."

"A *boy*," Jessica added. Kelly tried to protest, but Jessica raised her hand to stop her. "His name is Nicholas Morrow, and he's the *most* gorgeous hunk in town. He's dying to meet you. . . ."

Dazed, Kelly stared at her cousin as she rattled on at breakneck speed.

"He's rich, handsome, smart—you name it. He's taking a year off before he goes to college, is working in his father's computer company, and he drives a Jeep—he's kind of the rugged individualist type—"

"Jessica!" Alice Wakefield interrupted from the front seat. "I think poor Kelly is getting

11

dizzy. Why don't you let her find out a few things about Nicholas on her own."

Kelly shook her head slowly. "He sounds pretty—nice," she said in an awed voice. She turned to look at Elizabeth. "What's the catch? Doesn't he have a girlfriend?"

"No catch," Elizabeth said with a smile. Her eyes grew serious as she added, "The only thing is, his sister died a little while ago."

Kelly gasped with horror. "What happened?"

A quiver of emotion passed across Elizabeth's face. "Regina got in with a bad crowd when she was feeling upset about something. She went to the wrong kind of party. . . ." Elizabeth's voice faded out, and she turned to look out the window for a moment.

Jessica cleared her throat. "She tried some cocaine, and it did something weird to her heart. She went into a coma and died."

Kelly shook her head, her throat dry. "I don't think I should—"

"No, it's OK," Elizabeth interrupted, a soft smile on her face. "Nicholas wants to meet you. He really does."

"Are you sure?"

"Yes. Positive. And, look! We're home."

Surprised, Kelly turned to look through Jessica's window. They had stopped in front of a split-level ranch house. A golden labrador retriever was standing on the front steps, wagging his tail so hard that his whole body swayed from side to side.

"Who's *that*?" Kelly asked, laughing.

"And what's he doing outside when no one's home?" Mr. Wakefield asked.

Jessica looked sheepish for a moment. "I guess I forgot to put him in the house." Then she brightened. "But doesn't Prince Albert make a great welcoming committee?" Before her father could comment, Jessica was out of the car.

Scrambling out after Jessica, Kelly stood looking up at the house that would be her home for the next two months. Her aunt climbed out of the car and stood beside her, putting one arm across her shoulders.

"Welcome home, Kelly," Mrs. Wakefield said with a loving squeeze. "Welcome to Sweet Valley."

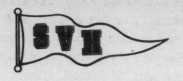

Two

"Here, wear this," Jessica suggested. She pulled her favorite denim miniskirt out of a drawer and handed it to Kelly. It was Kelly's first day at Sweet Valley High, and Jessica wanted her cousin to look her best.

Kelly shook her head. "No, I don't think so, Jessica."

"But why not?"

"Well—" Kelly looked hesitant, then broke into a huge grin, "I've got one just like it myself." She went over to the extra chest Mr. Wakefield had put in the room.

Jessica hopped onto her bed and crossed her legs. She watched as her cousin pulled out a skirt almost identical to her own, and then got an inspiration. "I know—we'll *all* dress exactly the same, like Liz and I used to in fifth grade. It'll be hysterical."

14

Her eyes twinkling, Kelly nodded and stepped into her skirt. "I've got a great pink shirt," she added as she turned back to the chest. "It's like the one you were wearing on Saturday."

"This is a riot." Jessica laughed as she wriggled her skirt over her head, then pulled on a purple T-shirt. "Hey, Liz!"

Elizabeth's head appeared in the doorway of the bathroom that connected the twins' rooms. "You called?" she replied.

Jessica turned to Kelly, and both girls burst into hysterics. Elizabeth was wearing her own denim skirt and a blue T-shirt almost identical to Jessica's.

"What's the joke?" Elizabeth asked in surprise. Her eyes went from Jessica to Kelly and back again, and then she smiled. "Great minds think alike, huh?"

"You're not kidding!" Jessica yanked open a drawer and pulled out a pair of purple crew socks. "It's kind of dumb, but it's pretty funny, too, don't you think?"

Soon the three girls were dressed—in denim skirts, T-shirts, colorful socks, and sneakers. With an appraising glance at Kelly and Elizabeth, Jessica shrugged and pulled her hair back into a ponytail. Usually she liked to wear it loose, but the "triplets" look was too funny not to make it complete.

"I'm ready," she said. She moved over to her

15

full-length mirror and then motioned Kelly and Elizabeth to stand next to her. They stood with their arms across each other's shoulders. Even though Kelly didn't look exactly like her and Elizabeth, Jessica realized the identical outfits made the similarities much more obvious. Their eyes met in the mirror, and they all started giggling.

"Nobody's going to *believe* this," Jessica declared. "They'll all think they've got something wrong with their eyes."

As soon as the girls had gotten home on Saturday, they had decided to keep Kelly as a surprise and spring her on Sweet Valley High first thing Monday morning. So far, no one else had met her, not even Cara Walker or Lila Fowler, Jessica's best friends, or Jeffrey French or Enid Rollins.

On Sunday they had lounged around the pool behind the house all day, filling Kelly in on the important details about life in Sweet Valley: who were the nicest teachers; which students were going out with whom and why, and for how long; where the best stores were; as well as telling her dozens of stories about the people Kelly would meet. By bedtime the twins were as excited as Kelly about her first day at school.

"If we're going to eat breakfast, we'd better hurry," Elizabeth warned, glancing at her watch.

"Kelly has to check in at the office before homeroom."

Kelly stopped in the middle of the room. "Shouldn't we make our beds before we go?" she asked hesitantly. "I mean, look at this room. . . ."

In less than two days Jessica's impeccably tidy room had returned to its original state: a disaster zone. Kelly's clothes were only half-unpacked, and most of Jessica's clothes were out of the closet again from a marathon wardrobe-comparing session. And with the extra bed and chest, there was even less room than before for the same volume of mess.

Jessica surveyed the damage; it would take hours to clean up. She shook her head. "Nah," she said. "What's the use?"

Her sister caught her eye and snorted. "OK, OK." Jessica laughed. "I know it's a mess again, but that's just the way I am. Let's go."

"All right!"

After a quick breakfast of cereal and fruit, they headed outside. As Jessica opened the door on the driver's side of the twins' red Fiat convertible, Kelly stopped.

"This is a two-seater," she said.

"Clever girl, this cousin of ours," Jessica said to Elizabeth. She nodded to the passenger seat. "Come on, it's no big deal. We've doubled up lots of times. You can sit on Liz's lap."

"She's so generous with other people's laps," Elizabeth commented under her breath.

Kelly looked blankly from Elizabeth to Jessica and back again. Then she laughed, shrugged, and climbed onto Elizabeth's lap.

Moments later they were driving down the tree-lined streets of Sweet Valley. Jessica narrowed her eyes with pleasure as the wind whipped around them, and she smiled over at Kelly. Her cousin was grinning from ear to ear. They pulled up the sweeping driveway of the high school, and Jessica deftly maneuvered the sports car into a space in the parking lot.

"Not exactly door-to-door service, but here it is, madame."

Elizabeth released the safety belt she had drawn around her cousin and herself, and Kelly scrambled out. Elizabeth heaved an exaggerated sigh of relief. "You weigh a ton, Kelly Bates."

"Sorry," Kelly replied sweetly. Her eyes glowed with an impish twinkle, and she turned to look at the school.

Jessica hopped out, too, and stooped down for a moment to check out her appearance in the side-view mirror. Over her shoulder she caught a glimpse of Bill Chase, Sweet Valley's resident surf champion, driving his car into the lot. She straightened quickly.

"Look, there's Bill," she whispered, leaning

18

across the Fiat's hood toward Kelly and Elizabeth. They both looked off in his direction with puzzled frowns. "Don't you get it?" Jessica demanded.

With a shrug Elizabeth said, "Actually, no."

Jessica leaned farther across the hood, grinning with anticipation. "Let's see if he notices us."

A grin spread across Elizabeth's face, and she erupted in a bubbling laugh. "It would be something if he *doesn't* notice us."

Jessica linked arms with Kelly and started marching toward Bill. Elizabeth ran to catch up with them.

"Hi, Bill," Jessica called brightly as the three of them approached Bill's car.

The muscular sun-bronzed surfer paused for a moment as he looked out his window. "Hey," he drawled, his eyes opening wide as he stared at them. "Awesome," he declared.

Grinning serenely, Jessica led Kelly and Elizabeth on without stopping. Once past, they started laughing.

"Well, I guess he did notice," Kelly said. "If we produce that kind of reaction from him, what's next?"

"You'll see," Jessica said. Up ahead on the steps were Ms. Dalton, their French teacher, and Caroline Pearce, one of the twins' classmates. They trooped up the stairs in a row.

19

"So you see," Caroline was saying as they walked up, "I was—" She spotted them out of the corner of her eye and whirled around, her mouth open in surprise.

Ms. Dalton turned, too, and her eyebrows flew up. She looked at them in silence for a moment and then grinned mischievously. "Well, *mon dieu*—to coin a phrase. You must be Kelly Bates. Welcome to Sweet Valley High."

Caroline finally found her voice. "I can't be-lieve it! I just can't be-*lieve* it," she gushed, her green eyes darting from Jessica to Kelly to Elizabeth. "This is just incredible. You look so— I mean, sure, you can tell the difference, but still! And you're all dressed the same, too! I can't *believe* this," she repeated.

Kelly met Jessica's eyes and winked. "I guess I'm going to be hot news for a while."

Already half a dozen girls were crowded around them, clamoring over Kelly, saying how unbelievable the family resemblance was and eagerly listing the ways in which Kelly was different: her hair was a shade darker and not as wavy, her eyes were green instead of aqua, her cheekbones were higher, her face narrower. Kelly nodded and smiled and tried to catch people's names as they introduced themselves.

"OK, you guys," Jessica announced in a businesslike tone over the busy chatter. "We really have to go—Kelly has to register for school."

Kelly turned with a look of total amazement. "I guess we look a little bit alike, huh?" She laughed.

Taking her cousin's arm in a firm grip, Jessica nodded. "I know. Tomorrow you'd better come in disguise."

Kelly leaned her forehead against her locker and winced as she tried to remember her new combination. Twenty-zero-fifteen. Or was it fifteen-zero-twenty? Her head was spinning from her first day: new faces, new classes, finding her way around. If she could just remember her combination, she would consider the day a success.

She tried both, and the lock dropped open on the second attempt. She shook her head and opened the locker.

"Hi, Kelly."

Turning, she saw two girls walking past her down the hall. One was a petite blond, the other dark-haired with flawless skin. She smiled in return but was afraid to be too daring with names. She was pretty sure they were Jean West and Sandra Bacon, but she was definitely not sure which one was which. "Hi," she called back lamely.

Just then, Elizabeth rounded a corner and hurried toward her.

"Boy, am I glad to see you!" Kelly leaned back against the lockers with relief.

"Feeling a little overwhelmed?"

For an answer Kelly just rolled her eyes.

"Come on," Elizabeth said, smiling. "I'll show you the newspaper office. I have to add something to my column anyway. A friend of mine, Robin Wilson, just told me she's going to be in a four-county diving championship."

Nodding, Kelly put away her books and shut the locker. She smoothed her skirt, then eyed her cousin skeptically. "OK—I'm as ready as I'm ever going to be, I guess."

"You'll be fine." Elizabeth led her down the hallway, adding, "You did meet Mr. Collins today, right? You must have him for English."

Kelly recalled the handsome young teacher and remembered how surprised she had been when he entered the room. He looked more like a movie star than an English teacher!

"I wish I had him for every class," Kelly confessed with a lopsided grin. "One period a day is not enough."

They came to a halt outside a door labeled *The Oracle*, and Elizabeth gave her a knowing nod. "Believe me, he's one of the best teachers here—he's really a great guy. *And* he's the newspaper adviser, too," she added, arching her eyebrows provocatively.

"Whoa—look out!" Kelly exclaimed. "I'm about to become a reporter."

Elizabeth laughed and pushed open the door, and Kelly followed her inside. Seated at a big table with a stack of papers in front of her was a serious-looking girl with short, dark blond hair. She looked up with an inquiring smile that changed to instant recognition.

"Hi, Liz. Hi, Kelly—we met at lunch. I'm Penny Ayala."

"The Big Chief," Elizabeth supplied.

"Make that editor in chief extraordinaire," put in a girl at the back of the room. She turned, her Indian-print skirt swirling around her. "Hi, I'm Olivia Davidson. I'm in your chemistry class."

Kelly gave them both a friendly smile and looked around her with interest. The newspaper office was very much like the one in her Tucson school—battered gray file cabinets, dog-eared reference books, and cartoons and clippings all over the walls. Several typewriters were lined up against one wall.

She nodded in admiration. "Nice cozy place you have here."

"We call it home," Penny replied breezily. "Did you work on the paper in your old school?"

"Not on a regular basis, but I do like to write." Kelly perched on the edge of the table while

Elizabeth crossed to one of the typewriters and dumped her book bag.

"Maybe you can do something for the paper while you're here, then."

"Sure!"

"You should ask her what the assignment is before you accept," Elizabeth warned. "Penny can be pretty brutal."

"You keep out of this, Wakefield," the editor retorted in a mock haughty voice. She gave Kelly a wink. "You're in a unique position, living with the infamous Wakefield twins. How about writing an exposé: 'The Secret Life of Elizabeth and Jessica—The True Story.' "

Olivia let out a peal of laughter. "Sounds like a TV miniseries."

"I don't know," Kelly said, rubbing her chin thoughtfully. "I don't want my cousins to hate me."

"Well, OK," Penny continued. She propped her chin up in her hands. "You used to live in Sweet Valley when you were little, right? How about a story on how the town has changed since you've been gone?"

Kelly dropped her eyes quickly. There was no way to explain that in many ways her early years in Sweet Valley were simply blank pages in her memory. Family life when her father was still with them—that was what she couldn't really recall. Aunt Alice, Uncle Ned, Elizabeth, Jessica, and Steven—she remembered them perfectly. But every time she tried to call up a picture of living with her mother and father together, she just drew a blank.

Of course, she had dozens of happy memories of her father since then. She remembered vividly every time he visited her or took her away for a weekend. He was funny and loving and generous and understanding. Whenever she thought about what she was missing by not having him around full-time, she felt an overwhelming surge of resentment against her mother. It was just impossible to understand how her mother could have divorced him.

"Kelly?"

"Oh!" She jumped nervously and looked up to meet Elizabeth's puzzled gaze. She glanced at Penny, who was waiting for an answer.

"Sorry. I was too young," she confessed, suddenly feeling awkward and uncomfortable. Her gaze shifted uncertainly back to Elizabeth, who gave her a supportive smile. "I could do a stranger's view—something like that."

Penny shrugged. "Sure. Try some kind of angle, though—more than just first impressions, OK?"

"No problem," Kelly agreed with a grateful sigh. She could feel her heart pounding heavily, the way it always did when she thought about her parents' divorce. "I'll get started on it right now."

Jumping off the table, she pulled a legal pad toward her and began jotting down notes for her article. Gradually her heart slowed to its normal pace, and she felt herself relaxing again. She glanced up once at Elizabeth, who was typing out her column. Their eyes met briefly, and Elizabeth frowned, asking a silent question. Her cheeks flushing, Kelly dropped her eyes without a word.

Three

After dinner the next day, Jessica slipped into Elizabeth's room and shut the door quietly behind her. Elizabeth looked up from her journal expectantly, waiting for her twin to speak.

"Liz, I have to tell you something," Jessica whispered, giving her a meaningful look.

Elizabeth raised her eyebrows. "Sounds pretty serious," she replied lightly.

"It is—I think. I mean, maybe it's none of my business. . . ." Frowning, Jessica sat down on the edge of Elizabeth's bed and twisted her fingers together. She met her sister's eyes. "Tell me if you think I should say something to her about it."

"Who? About what?" Elizabeth prompted.

Jessica shrugged. "Well—last night Kelly had some kind of awful nightmare."

"What?" Immediately concerned, Elizabeth sat

down next to Jessica and looked intently into her face. "What—I mean, did she say anything about it? What was it about?"

Jessica shook her head emphatically. "Well, I asked her, but she just wouldn't say. She *really* didn't want to talk about it." Rolling her eyes, she added, "But it must have been terrible. She was crying in her sleep, and it woke me up."

"Oh, no! That's *awful*. Poor Kelly."

"Do you think we should—I don't know—say something to her?"

Elizabeth frowned. Talking things over was usually the best policy. But if it was too painful for Kelly . . . "Well, if she didn't want to talk about it, I don't think we should push it. I guess we should just make sure she's happy here. It's probably some kind of anxiety about being in a new place, being accepted—you know?"

Jessica looked doubtful. "If you say so."

"That must be it," Elizabeth said firmly. Her heart ached at the thought of her cousin being so worried that she had nightmares. "We'll just have to make everything easy on her—and remember: nothing bad about Uncle Greg."

"I haven't said anything!" Jessica protested, looking injured.

"I know. I'm just reminding you. Kelly definitely doesn't need any criticism of him on top of everything else."

28

Jessica shrugged. "I guess. Anyway, don't you think we should be heading for the Dairi Burger?"

Elizabeth shot a quick glance at her watch. "You're right. Nicholas is meeting us there in twenty minutes."

They headed downstairs, calling for Kelly. "You know," Jessica muttered, "it's pretty mind-boggling to think *I'm* helping to fix Nicholas Morrow up with someone else. Even if she is my cousin."

"What a saint you are, Jessica," Elizabeth replied. "Now let's get Kelly and get out of here."

The Dairi Burger was unusually crowded for a Tuesday night. The pinball machines and video games were beeping and ringing at one end of the long room, and a muffled roar rose from the crowded tables and booths. At the counter a line of people edged forward to order hamburgers, chili-dogs, milk shakes, and french fries.

"OK, Kelly, this is your big chance," Jessica hissed, craning her neck to see the door.

"Jessica, come on!" Blushing, Kelly looked down at the table and toyed with her chocolate shake in embarrassment.

Elizabeth looked at Kelly sympathetically. "Don't worry—he's easy to talk to. Really." As she raised her head, she caught sight of Nicholas Morrow near the door. He glanced around, spotted them, and waved. Then he pointed to the counter, meaning he wanted to get some food first.

He joined them a few minutes later, carrying a loaded tray. "Hi." Nicholas slid into the booth next to Elizabeth and held out his hand to Kelly. "I'm Nicholas. I could have guessed you were Liz and Jess's cousin. How are you?"

"Fine, thanks," Kelly replied with a shy smile as she shook his hand. "It's nice to meet you." Her eyes darted to Elizabeth for a split second, and Elizabeth read the surprise and pleasure she saw there. Nicholas was everything Jessica had said—extremely handsome, with dark hair and startlingly vivid green eyes. He was friendly and casual, too, and instantly put Kelly at ease.

"I hope you girls don't mind if I eat dinner," Nicholas said with a grin, nodding at the burger and Coke he had brought to the table. "I just came from work, and I'm starving."

"Your father makes you work this late?" Jessica asked in a horrified tone.

He laughed and shook his head. "We're going camping up in the mountains for a long weekend, and we have to get a lot of work done before we can go. See, I work at my father's computer company," he explained to Kelly. "He's not really a slave driver."

Kelly's eyes shone. "It must be great to be

30

able to work with your own father," she said, resting her chin in her hand. "I wish I could."

"What does your dad do?"

"Right now he's a consultant, and he travels a lot," Kelly told him eagerly. "He lives a few towns away now, but we used to live in Sweet Valley. He's really fun to be with. I think he's great," she added with a laugh.

Nicholas returned her smile. "It shows."

Elizabeth and Jessica exchanged a look across the table. Kelly's opinion of her father was certainly different from Mrs. Wakefield's, and Elizabeth wondered why. Mrs. Wakefield had known Greg Bates very well and said he was selfish, hot-tempered, and irresponsible. But he *was* Kelly's father. Kelly had spent a lot of time with him, and *she* obviously thought he was perfect. Frowning, Elizabeth jammed her straw into the crushed ice at the bottom of her root beer. It just didn't make sense.

"Here's a picture of him," Kelly went on as she dug into her purse. She pulled out her wallet and opened it to a photograph. Nicholas took it with a polite smile, and Elizabeth peered over his shoulder.

"He's really handsome," Elizabeth said, startled by the face in the picture: black hair, a roguish, self-mocking smile, dark eyes, and an air of disarming charm. "I'd forgotten what he looks like, it's been so long."

Jessica pulled the photo toward her. "Let me—wow! You're not kidding," she exclaimed, looking at Kelly with admiration. "Too bad he's too old for me!" she said, her dimple showing.

With a laugh Nicholas popped a french fry into his mouth. "I'd like to hear more about him," he said, smiling at Kelly. "He sounds like a great guy."

"Oh, he is!" Kelly took a sip of her milk shake and looked dreamily at her father's picture. "He'll be back in town at the end of next week. He's coming back from Europe just to be with me on my birthday. Isn't that incredible? I can't wait to see him."

"I don't blame you. What's your mom like?"

Kelly's smile faded, and she shrugged noncommittally. "You know. Just a typical mom."

"I guess I know what that means," Nicholas said, laughing. "Hey—would you like to go to a costume party with me at the country club a week from Saturday? That is, if it fits in with your plans. It should be pretty good."

Kelly dropped her eyes shyly and sneaked a glance at Elizabeth. Her cousin gave her a heartfelt smile. For Elizabeth, hearing Nicholas ask her cousin to the dance was a double triumph. Not only did it mean that Kelly had made an instant hit, but it also meant that Nicholas was finally coming out of the shell he had been hiding in since Regina's tragic death.

"Sure, I'd love to. Thanks, Nicholas."

"It's my pleasure." With a contented sigh Nicholas pushed away his empty plate and looked at Jessica and Elizabeth. "You're both going, aren't you?"

Jessica nodded. "Lila asked us as her guests," she explained. "There's no way we would miss it. I *love* costume parties."

For a moment Nicholas regarded the three girls appraisingly. A slow smile broke over his handsome face. "You know," he said, "you three should go as a trio of some sort."

"What, like the Three Little Pigs or something?" Jessica asked.

Kelly giggled. "Now, there's an idea."

"I'm serious! Why not? Kelly looks enough like you two for it to work."

"Please," Jessica insisted in a pained tone. "We're a little old for that."

"It's really not a bad idea," Elizabeth said thoughtfully, meeting Nicholas's eyes. She laughed. "Besides, we did it yesterday at school. It's really a great idea."

Nicholas nodded enthusiastically. "Sure, just play up the similarities between you two and Kelly. It would be lots of fun. Don't you think?" he asked, appealing to Kelly. There was a hopeful, boyish look in his eyes.

His smile was impossible to resist. She nodded without hesitation. "Yeah, it would be fun. As long as Jessica agrees."

All eyes turned to Jessica, who pouted. "I was going to go as something really wild. I found a bunch of huge ostrich plumes at a tag sale, and I wanted to use them."

"The Three Musketeers!" Kelly cried, grabbing Jessica's arm. "They had huge feathers in their hats, didn't they?"

As Jessica frowned thoughtfully, Nicholas shook his head. "I was thinking more along the lines of the Three Blind Mice. You could all wear mouse suits and paint whiskers on your faces—and hold on to each other's tails."

"Nicholas! That's ridiculous." Elizabeth let out a peal of laughter.

"Well, let's think about it some more," Jessica said finally. "Maybe going as triplets *is* a good idea. There—satisfied?" she asked, looking at Nicholas.

He chuckled. "Never." Glancing at his watch, he let out a sigh. "Oh, wow. I have to go. It was really great meeting you, Kelly," he continued, rising to his feet. He smiled regretfully. "I'm just sorry I have to leave so early. I'll give you a call about the dance."

Kelly's eyes glowed as she looked up at him. "Sure. Thanks for asking me. It was nice to meet you, too."

" 'Bye, Liz. 'Bye, Jess. I'll see you soon."

Nicholas turned and waved, then maneuvered his way through the crowd. All three girls followed him with their eyes until he disappeared out the door.

"Well?" Jessica eagerly asked her cousin. "What did you think of him? Isn't he *amazing*?"

"Hmm . . ." Kelly used her straw to stir her milk shake. "Well . . ."

Elizabeth laughed suddenly. "That's enough acting, Kelly. You don't fool anyone."

"Oh, yeah?" She laughed back. Kelly couldn't stop smiling, and she shook her head in wonder. "He's really nice," she admitted shyly, looking from Jessica to Elizabeth and back again. "*Really* nice."

Jessica sat back and gestured grandly with one hand. "There! What did I tell you? *And* he obviously likes you, if asking you to the costume party after knowing you *five* minutes means anything. This could be the start of an epic romance!"

There was a pause as they all remembered that Kelly's visit was only temporary. Elizabeth gave Kelly a rueful smile. "It's too bad you aren't staying forever. I wish you could."

"Actually—" Kelly made circles on their table with one finger. Then she squared her shoulders and looked up. "Actually, I've decided to stay."

"What?"

She nodded emphatically. "When my dad comes back, I'm going to tell him I want to live with him instead of Mom—and maybe he'll be willing to move back to Sweet Valley. After all, he's only a few towns away now. No way am I going back to Mom and the guy she's marrying and his kids!"

Elizabeth swallowed hard and glanced furtively at her twin. Jessica looked as shocked and uneasy as Elizabeth felt. From all they had heard, Kelly's father didn't sound like the sort of person who would just settle down and be a responsible parent. And their aunt's plan was for Kelly to grow used to the idea of her new marriage, not to turn her back on it!

"Uh, Kelly? Don't you think you should discuss that with Aunt Laura?" Elizabeth asked, feeling her cheeks warm. "It's kind of a big decision," she added lamely.

But Kelly's chin jutted out stubbornly, and she set her mouth in a determined line. "No," she declared. "I never liked Tuscon, and it's all Mom's fault anyway that I haven't been able to grow up with my own father. She wouldn't even ever let me come back here to visit him! He always had to come all the way to Tucson. I'm almost seventeen, and I think I'm old enough to make that kind of decision by myself.

"Besides," she added, dropping her eyes, "Mom doesn't understand me, and I don't think she's fair. We just never get along—I mean, being here with you guys is so much better!"

"Well, if you do stay—" Jessica faltered. She shot an uncertain look at Elizabeth. "If you do, that'd be great."

Kelly nodded, and clenched her hands together on the table. "I'm not going back to Mom," she repeated in a low, intense voice. "I'm staying with my father."

Four

Jessica bounced a tennis ball on her racket and shot a quick glance over the net at Kelly. "Prepare to die," she drawled. She tossed the ball above her head and, with a practiced flip of her wrist, brought her racket smashing across it.

"Net!" Kelly called, giving Jessica an arch smile as she crouched down into position again.

"OK, OK." Jessica brushed the back of her hand across her forehead and squinted against the late-afternoon sun. It was hot, and the game wasn't going the way she wanted. She popped up another ball, and her racket whistled through the air a second time.

"Double fault. Game. My service."

For a moment Jessica stood with her hands on her hips and looked across the court at her cousin. Then she shook her head. "I thought you said you were an *average* player, Kelly. And here you are making me double-fault every five seconds and breaking my serve. I might as well go home and do my homework."

Kelly shrugged and hit the toe of one tennis shoe with the strings of her racket. Then she gave Jessica another arch smile. "Did I say that? Are you sure I said that?"

"Just play, Bates," Jessica said, trying to sound serious, sidestepping to the baseline. "Your serve. And *don't* you try to ace me."

Laughing, Kelly shook her head and pulled a ball from the pocket of her shorts, bounced it a few times on the court, and lofted it into the air as she swung her racket back. It whizzed across the net, and Jessica met it with a startled yelp as she backhanded it clumsily into the chain-link fence. A vibrating *clang* shuddered through the silence.

"Kelly!" Half-laughing, half-gasping, Jessica flipped her racket over her shoulder.

"Sorry, Jess," Kelly replied with a sheepish grin. "I'm sorry. Really."

Jessica studied her cousin's face for a moment. When she had suggested a tennis game after school, Jessica hadn't bargained for such a crushing defeat! But Kelly was good, and Jessica loved a challenging game.

Besides, Kelly was having so much fun. Her eyes were sparkling, and her cheeks were flushed with excitement. Jessica's mind went back to her conversation with Elizabeth about Kelly's nightmare. At this rate Kelly shouldn't have any doubts about being accepted and having a good time.

"OK," Jessica said in a warning tone as she picked up her racket. "But you have to promise you won't try to kill me."

Kelly giggled. "I promise." She drew a deep breath, tossed up another ball, and slammed a perfect ace over the net.

Before Jessica could speak, the sound of languid applause reached them. Spinning around quickly, Jessica saw Kirk Anderson sitting on the bench beyond the fence, his long legs stretched out in front of him.

"Oh, it's you," she said in disgust, turning away.

When Kirk had made his first appearance at Sweet Valley High a few months earlier, a lot of girls had been taken in by his dark good looks. His jet-black hair fell in a tousled wave across his forehead, and his deep-set eyes seemed to show a glimpse of the fire inside.

But the reality of Kirk Anderson could be summed up by Jessica's nickname for him: Kirk the Jerk. He was arrogant, rude, swaggering, insensitive, and immature, and it had only taken her and a number of other girls at Sweet Valley a few short days to figure it out.

At one point he had been the ringmaster of a

cruel practical joke against Penny Ayala, and Jessica had teamed up with her twin to get back at him. They had led him to believe that a beautiful young fashion model, Erica Hall, was their cousin and that she would agree to go on a blind date with him. He had gone to a big school dance alone, waiting in vain for Erica to appear.

"Yes, it's me, Jessica," he drawled as he clasped his hands behind his neck and tossed his mane of black hair back off his forehead. He appraised Kelly with a lingering glance. "Your favorite person in the whole world."

"Just ignore him, Kelly," Jessica said in a scornful tone.

"You know," Kirk continued, staring meaningfully at Kelly, "Jessica and Elizabeth once tried to set me up with their beautiful cousin. I guess you were tied up—that's why you couldn't make it."

"What—I don't—" Flustered, Kelly looked from Kirk to Jessica and back again. Her cheeks were tinged with pink, and she toyed unconsciously with the ends of her windblown hair.

Jessica turned her back on Kirk deliberately and folded her arms. "Come on, Kelly. Your serve."

"So I figure you owe me an apology, Cousin," Kirk went on, his voice slow and husky.

Kelly walked uncertainly toward the fence as

though pulled by a magnet. She gave him a hesitant smile. "What are you talking about?"

He rose from the bench and strolled nonchalantly to the fence opposite her. He twined the fingers of one hand through the links and gave Kelly another appraising glance. "I'm talking about you and me going out sometime. It's only fair."

"Oh, give it up, Kirk," Jessica exploded. "That's the most nauseating line I ever heard."

Kirk narrowed his eyes at her. "I wasn't talking to you." Smiling again, he turned back to Kelly. "How about it? Want to grab some dinner at the Dairi Burger with me?"

"Well . . ." For a moment Kelly hesitated, her cheeks flaming.

With growing horror Jessica realized that Kelly was attracted to Kirk. It was obvious by the self-conscious way Kelly kept shifting from one foot to the other, her eyes darting to Kirk's handsome features.

How could Kelly not see what a total jerk he was? Jessica wondered.

"How about it?" Kirk repeated.

"Well—sure. That is—" Kelly turned to Jessica hopefully. "You don't mind, do you, Jess? I mean—we're nearly finished with this set."

Heaving a sigh of exasperation, Jessica rolled her eyes and shrugged. "Yeah, sure. I don't care. You were winning, anyway." *And you'll find out soon enough what Kirk is all about,* she thought.

"Oh—great. OK," Kelly said. "I'll see you later, then, Jess. And you'll tell Aunt Alice I won't be home for dinner?"

"Yeah, sure," Jessica said grumpily, crossing to the sideline and zipping her racket into its case. She paused for a moment to give Kirk a withering look. He grinned back triumphantly, further infuriating her. With another snort of disgust, she strode off the court.

"She'll find out soon enough what a total conceited pig he is," she said aloud as she opened the door of the Fiat. "And I won't even have to say a word."

"I'm telling you, Liz, it was totally unreal." Jessica hung facedown over the end of her bed and examined the fringe of blond hair in front of her eyes. "Give me those scissors, would you?"

Stretching across Kelly's bed, Elizabeth grabbed a pair of scissors and tossed them to her twin. As she went back to fondling Prince Albert's silky ears, she frowned. She had been completely taken aback when she heard Kelly was having dinner with Kirk Anderson. "Well, don't worry about it. When Kelly walks through that door, she'll realize that she made a big mistake."

43

"Yeah, right," Jessica agreed. She isolated a split end and snipped it off. "She probably regretted it by the time they ordered their burgers. I mean, how long can a sane person stand to listen to Kirk the Jerk?"

Elizabeth grew thoughtful again. "Jess? You don't think she was serious about not going home to Aunt Laura, do you? It seems like her feelings about her parents are exactly the reverse of what they should be—it's strange."

"Don't ask me," Jessica said. "I don't get it at all. I just hope Kelly doesn't go and tell Mom. She'd have a fit if she heard that."

The door opened quietly, and both girls looked up as Kelly came inside. Elizabeth waited in suspense for Kelly to say something about Kirk. Kelly propped her tennis racket against the bureau and sat down next to Jessica at the end of the bed, and Prince Albert thumped his tail in welcome.

"Hi, Kelly," Jessica said encouragingly.

Kelly met Jessica's eyes and sighed. "Hi."

"Did you have a good time?" Elizabeth's voice resonated with doubt.

Kelly nodded vigorously. "Yes—Kirk is a really nice guy."

Jessica stared. "*Nice?*" she repeated, struggling upright and sitting on her knees.

"Sure—oh!" Kelly broke off and crossed her legs under her. "I guess you think he's sort of insensitive and thoughtless. He told me some people think that about him—but that he's tried to change lately." She leaned down to tickle Prince Albert's neck.

Over her head Jessica and Elizabeth stared at each other in disbelief. Kirk Anderson would have to do some pretty drastic changing to be anything but insensitive and thoughtless. From what Elizabeth knew of him, she wouldn't be surprised if he used a tactic like that as an insurance policy. He would expect Elizabeth and Jessica to tell Kelly about his dirty tricks, so he was one step ahead of them.

Elizabeth cleared her throat. "Well. That's interesting."

"Interesting," Jessica echoed dryly.

Kelly nodded. "He's really sorry about the way he treated people when he first came to Sweet Valley," she explained eagerly. "He says it was because he was so shy and afraid of being rejected."

"Shy? That's not the Kirk Anderson *I* know," Jessica said sarcastically. She leaned back against her pillows and propped one leg up across the other knee. Then she went back to hunting for split ends, as though dismissing the subject.

"He is sweet—and—and romantic. I guess you have to get to know him," Kelly continued softly as she undid the tabs on her tennis shoes.

Elizabeth said nothing. Instead, she curled

up on the floor next to Prince Albert and scratched absently behind his ears. She didn't think there was anything *to* say. If her cousin decided she liked Kirk Anderson, that was her business, not theirs. But she couldn't help wishing Kelly was a better judge of character.

"Well, *anyway*"—Jessica sighed dramatically, breaking the silence—"let's talk about our costumes. I've been thinking about it, and I really think the Three Musketeers is a good idea."

Kelly grimaced and pulled off her tennis socks. "But then we have to go as men—and wear beards and mustaches!" she pointed out, tossing her socks toward the hamper.

With a sudden chuckle Elizabeth added, "And I don't think they were blond, either."

"Well, I refuse to go as the Three Little Pigs," Jessica insisted, giving her twin a warning look.

Heaving an exasperated sigh, Elizabeth leaned back against Kelly's bed. "We have to agree on *something* if we're going as a trio. I think it was a great idea of Nicholas's. He just didn't know how long we would end up arguing about *which* trio!"

Kelly pushed herself up and paced across the room. Then she swung around and fixed Elizabeth with a pleading look. "Don't you think Nicholas just asked me to the party out of politeness? I mean, he doesn't even know me."

Elizabeth became very still. "Why do you ask?"

46

"Well . . ." Biting her lower lip, Kelly began pacing again and stopped by Jessica's bureau. She mumbled, "It's just that Kirk's family belongs to the country club, too, and he asked me to go with *him*, and I—I really want to."

"You're kidding!" Jessica gasped, her eyes wide.

Elizabeth sat up straight. "Kelly—you can't break a date with someone because you want to go with someone else. It's not right."

"I know that. But it's not like it was a real date with Nicholas. He just asked me as a favor to you!"

Elizabeth knew that Nicholas never played games like that. If he had asked Kelly out, it was because he liked her and wanted to.

She glanced nervously at her twin. It was clear that Jessica was baffled to think anyone could contemplate breaking a date with Nicholas Morrow in favor of Kirk Anderson.

"Well, I really don't think that's why he asked you," Elizabeth answered hesitantly. "But if you really want to go with Kirk, you should call Nicholas now and tell him, so he has a chance to ask someone else."

"You must think I'm awful." Kelly's voice quavered with emotion. "But I—I've never felt like this before. I like Kirk so much."

Shaking her head in disgust, Jessica met Elizabeth's look of consternation. Elizabeth sighed wearily and closed her eyes.

"Call Nicholas, then, please? He's a really good friend. Be fair."

"I will. I'll call him—soon."

An awkward silence filled Jessica's room. There was a tension between the twins and Kelly that hadn't been there before.

Jessica cleared her throat. "It's time for that movie on TV that I want to watch," she announced as she pushed herself up off her bed. She looked from Kelly to Elizabeth and stalked from the room.

Kelly raised her eyes to Elizabeth's face. She was obviously upset and ashamed of herself—but she was also obviously being pulled both ways. With a pitiful shrug she shook her head. "Sorry."

Five

"What's this for—thirty-five dollars at Sport Zone?" Ned Wakefield ran one hand through his thick, wavy hair and held out a bill to his wife.

She crossed the den and took the bill. "Let me think. . . . Oh, right—Jessica's new cheer-leading uniform."

"And this one—from the Book Worm?"

Her eyes twinkling, Alice Wakefield suggested, "Books, maybe? Actually," she went on as she sank gracefully onto the couch, "I think that was for some reference books Liz needed."

Shaking his head, Mr. Wakefield sat back in his chair and tossed a pencil onto his desk. Neatly stacked piles of bills sat in front of him. "Teenagers! All I can say is, it's a good thing we didn't have triplets."

"Oh, Ned!" Mrs. Wakefield chuckled and

curled her legs up underneath her and took a sip of her coffee. "But really, I—"

Just then, the telephone rang shrilly. "I'll get it." Leaning forward, she picked it up. "Hello?"

"Alice? Hi, it's me."

Mrs. Wakefield's eyes lit up with pleasure. "Laura! Hi! How are you?" Covering the mouthpiece with her hand, she nodded toward her husband. "It's Laura!"

He grinned affectionately. "No kidding!" Pushing himself away from the desk, he added in a whisper, "I'll go get Kelly. I think they're all absorbed in a movie or something vitally important like that."

She shooed him out of the den with a mock scowl.

"So how's everything working out, Alice?"

"Just fine, don't worry—Kelly is a real pleasure to have around." Mrs. Wakefield took another sip of coffee.

"Oh, good. I was so unsure about this whole arrangement, but if it gives her a chance to get used to Tony and me and his kids . . ." Laura Bates paused before adding, "I never saw her so upset about anything as she was when I told her we wanted to get married. I think she looks at it as an attack on Greg."

"She just needs to settle down a bit," Mrs. Wakefield assured her sister, her voice more confident than she really felt. "But to tell you the truth, she hasn't really talked about your plans very much—at least not to Ned and me—so I can't say. But I'm sure she's talked to the twins."

"Oh, good. I know it's a big adjustment, but she's hardly spoken a complete sentence to me in a month."

Mrs. Wakefield looked up as her husband came back into the den, an expression of bewilderment on his face. A pang of alarm rippled through her, and she met his glance with a question in her eyes.

He shook his head silently.

"Alice?"

"Hold on a second, Laura." Covering the phone, Mrs. Wakefield frowned at her husband. "What? Is—"

"Kelly says she doesn't want to talk to her mother," he whispered hoarsely. He held out his hands and shrugged. "I don't know what to say. She just refuses to come to the phone."

For a moment Mrs. Wakefield stared at him. She knew Laura and Kelly's mother-daughter relationship was strained, but this was unexpected.

"Alice?"

"Oh, sorry, Laura," Alice Wakefield said. "Listen, Kelly and the girls are watching a movie, and apparently something absolutely crucial is happening that she can't miss. Can she call you tomorrow?"

"Of course—I understand," Laura Bates answered after a pause. "Tell her I love her."

"I will. I'll talk to you soon. 'Bye."

" 'Bye." There was a click, and the dial tone sounded. Mrs. Wakefield hung up the phone and sighed. "This is all wrong. Kelly is such a sweet girl. She shouldn't feel this way about her mother."

Leaning against the edge of the desk, Mr. Wakefield folded his arms and nodded. "I know, sweetheart. It's really a shame."

"Oh, Ned." With another sigh she leaned her head back against the couch and rubbed her eyes. "I can't say I really blame Kelly for not understanding—I just wish Laura would stick up for herself and tell her the whole story."

"Well, she thinks she's being fair to Kelly, letting her come to her own conclusions."

"But she's *not* being fair! That's the point! Shielding Kelly doesn't justify hiding the truth about Greg. He did some terrible things, and *I* think Kelly is old enough to know that— she deserves to know it."

Mr. Wakefield nodded sadly. "But it's what Laura thinks that matters, sweetheart. Kelly is her daughter, and we've promised to follow her rules while Kelly's here."

"I know, Ned." Mrs. Wakefield shook her head bleakly and stared into the bottom of her coffee cup. "But it's still wrong."

Kelly pulled a plate of tuna salad onto her tray and hurried after Jessica. "Are you serious about that necklace? I only want to borrow it. You don't have to give it to me, you know."

"No problem, Kelly," Jessica replied with a smile. "I really want you to have it. Come on, there's Lila and Cara. But remember—don't tell them what our costumes are going to be. They'll probably try to worm it out of you."

As Kelly followed her cousin through the cafeteria, she felt a rush of gratitude—and determination. She was definitely not going back to Tuscon. She was staying in Sweet Valley. With a decisive nod, she slipped into a chair across from Lila Fowler.

"Hey, Lila, is that a new belt?" Jessica asked as she picked up her slice of pizza.

Lila tossed her light brown hair back over her shoulders and glanced nonchalantly down at her waist. "Oh, this? Yes. Daddy just brought it back for me from Venice."

"Is that Venice, California?" Cara Walker asked with a mischievous twinkle in her dark eyes.

"Venice, *Italy*," Lila replied haughtily. "It's handmade Italian leather."

Kelly craned her neck to see Lila's belt and smiled admiringly. "It's really nice."

"My father always brings me incredibly expensive presents," Lila went on in a confidential tone. She tried to look modest as she added, "He just spoils me rotten."

Kelly toyed with her salad. "My father's in Europe now, too," she added softly. She knew she brought up the subject of her father a lot, but she couldn't help it. He was almost constantly in her thoughts these days.

"He is?" Lila sat up a little straighter and gave her an appraising look. "What's he doing there?"

"Well—" Kelly broke off and glanced up to meet Jessica's alert eyes. Puzzled, she realized that she wasn't quite sure what he was doing there. It had something to do with consulting. But she hated to admit she didn't know exactly what her father did.

"He's a consultant," she said, trying to sound confident. "Actually, when my mother left him, he was really broken up and quit his job," she added with a twinge of anger. "It took him a really long time to get back on his feet."

Cara leaned forward on her elbows. "Why did she leave him?" Instantly she realized that it was not her business, and she looked down at her plate in embarrassment. "Sorry, I didn't mean—"

"No, it's OK," Kelly said quickly. She was touched by Cara's concern for her father. Sighing, she shook her head and fingered the ends of her hair. "I've never known why. He's the

54

sweetest, most generous, wonderful father. He was always so good to my mother, and she broke his heart."

Jessica pulled her head back sharply in surprise. She looked askance at Kelly.

"Gosh, that sounds like a romance novel or something," Cara murmured, her eyes wide. She propped her chin up on one hand.

"Well, my mother isn't exactly a heroine," Kelly replied sourly. "She's a big pain. She never likes any of the guys I go out with, and she's always asking where I'm going, who I'll be with. That sort of stuff just makes me want to scream."

Jessica pressed her lips together and frowned at her pizza.

"But when I'm with Dad, he's really relaxed about rules and things. Whatever I want to do is fine with him. He never butts into my personal life at all. He trusts me completely."

"Do you ever get to see him?"

"Yes—but not enough," Kelly answered. "He lives near Sweet Valley, but for some reason my mother won't let me come out here. She's so mean! I miss my dad so much. But he'll be here next weekend for my birthday," she added with a glowing smile. "And he'll probably bring me a huge bunch of helium balloons or take me up in a glider or something. He's always doing these really off-the-wall things! I never know what to expect."

"Wow. He really sounds like a great father," Lila admitted. "All mine ever does is buy me stuff—he doesn't have very much imagination."

Kelly nodded vigorously. "I can remember once when I was maybe ten. He came to Tucson and took me to this carnival and let me have *anything* I wanted—cotton candy, ice cream, popcorn, soda. My mother would have told me I couldn't have any of it. He's the most wonderful father in the world. I'd rather live with him than my mother any day."

Jessica scowled. Kelly's complaints about her mother didn't impress her. All mothers acted that way, Jessica wanted to point out. That was just the way they were.

"I'm getting some ice cream," she announced suddenly, pushing herself up. She looked pointedly at Lila. "Come stand on line with me, OK?"

Surprised, Lila met Jessica's glance and narrowed her eyes. "Sure," she said, standing up.

"So what did you want to talk about?" Lila prompted as they joined the end of the food line.

Jessica grimaced. She had hoped Lila would get the silent message. She shook her head in confusion. "I don't know—it's weird." She shot a look over toward their table and lowered her voice. "I probably shouldn't tell you this, but my mother keeps talking about what a lousy guy Kelly's dad is. I mean, it sounds like my aunt left him because he was an absolute horror. But the guy Kelly is always talking about sounds like a totally different person."

Lila bit her lower lip and shrugged.

"And not only that," Jessica went on, frowning, "Kelly can't seem to stand her mother. Last night she called, and Kelly wouldn't even *talk* to her. Isn't that weird?"

They shuffled forward as the line inched ahead, and Lila shook her head. "I don't know what to tell you, Jess. It doesn't make any sense to me, either. So what are you wearing to the costume dance, anyway?" Lila continued without pausing to catch her breath.

Jessica rolled her eyes. Trust Lila to ignore a problem that didn't concern her. "You'll see," she replied airily. "No one's going to know until next Saturday night."

Kelly opened her eyes in the dark. Her heart pounding in her ears. How could something she couldn't even remember be so sickening, so overwhelmingly scary? A faint echo faded from her mind even though she tried to hold on to it. It sounded like a child's voice crying *"No, no, no!"* But then it was gone, and she couldn't be sure if she'd heard it at all.

All she could recall from the nightmare—even

seconds after she woke up—was a sensation of being in a small, enclosed space, like a cave. And of noises, awful screaming and crashing sounds, thundering and exploding all around and above her as she cowered in terror. It was horrible, frightening, and confusing.

Shaking, she curled up on her side and stared through the darkness toward Jessica's bed. Her cousin's breathing was slow and steady, and Kelly sighed in relief. If she had woken Jessica up again, it would have been awful. How could she admit to her cousin that she suffered from this paralyzing nightmare as often as she did?

Swallowing hard, Kelly bunched the pillow up under her cheek and tried to steady herself. If she could just relax and go to sleep, all the bad feelings would disappear. She fixed her eyes on the glow of the clock radio across the room. It was 3:16 A.M.

What does it mean? she wailed silently. Half of her wanted to know, and the other half didn't. What was it her nightmare was telling her? The book on dreams she had bought the previous year said that dreams were a window into the subconscious mind; that they represented fears and anxieties and tried to make sense out of daytime experiences. But why on earth did she have so many nightmares?

Just try to go to sleep, she commanded herself. *Don't even think about it.*

58

But she was completely awake. Sleep simply refused to come. She stared wide-eyed at the green glow of the clock: 3:32.

Things'll be better when Dad's back, she thought, moving her legs restlessly. *When Dad comes back, we can live together, and everything will be fine. I won't have any more nightmares.*

But as the clock changed noiselessly to 3:45, she suspected that that was just wishful thinking. She didn't believe her nightmares would ever go away.

Six

Kelly dropped an armload of textbooks into her canvas book bag, then hitched it up over her shoulder. "I *hate* trying to think of all the books I'll need over the weekend," she said. "I just know I'll forget something."

"I know what you mean. I always find out on Sunday afternoon that I left something critical at school!"

Kelly nodded and snapped her locker shut. "After you, madame," she said, gesturing.

"*Merci beaucoup!*"

As they turned down the hall, Kirk Anderson strolled into sight. Kelly's heart flip-flopped the moment she saw him, and she stole a glance at her cousin to gauge Elizabeth's reaction. Was it her imagination, or did Elizabeth seem irritated? If only her cousins would give him a chance, they would know how sincere and sensitive Kirk was behind his facade.

"Kelly!" Kirk stopped and leaned casually against a row of lockers to wait for them to catch up. He smiled confidently.

"Hi, Kirk," Kelly called.

Elizabeth maintained a stony silence. Kirk smiled even wider and then turned to Kelly. She couldn't help noticing the way his navy polo shirt brought out the color of his blue eyes.

"I've been thinking about you," Kirk said huskily.

Kelly blushed, but her eyes were glowing, and she couldn't stop smiling.

"Kelly, I'll wait for you in the car, OK?" Elizabeth said, starting down the hall.

Kelly shot her cousin a look of gratitude. "Thanks. I'll be right there."

"I don't think Liz is too crazy about me," Kirk observed as Elizabeth rounded the corner. His eyes sparkled mischievously as he added, "I guess she doesn't think I'm a very nice guy."

"Oh, come on!" Kelly exclaimed. "She just doesn't know you, that's all."

"Not like you, right?"

Kelly felt a flush creep over her cheeks as she met Kirk's bold look. He was certainly self-assured, she admitted to herself. But she liked that—it made her feel secure. With a challenging look in her eyes, she nodded. "Yes, I do."

"Good," Kirk drawled. He crossed his arms across his chest. "How about going to the Beach Disco with me tonight?"

Kelly let out a long breath and smiled. "Sure."

"Great. I'll pick you up at eight o'clock."

As Kirk sauntered away, Kelly hugged her arms around herself with excitement. She just knew that eight o'clock was going to be the starting point of a great evening. Smiling, she ran down the corridor toward the parking lot.

"There's a letter here for you, Kelly," Elizabeth said as she pulled the mail out of the mailbox. "Oh, no!" she cried as a tumble of catalogs and supermarket flyers cascaded to the ground. A long blue envelope fluttered out with them.

"I'll get it," Kelly replied quickly. Sifting rapidly through the pile of mail on the ground, Kelly pulled out the airmail envelope and sat back on her heels to rip it open. The thin paper made a crinkly noise as she ran her eyes over the letter.

Dear Princess,

You know I wouldn't miss your birthday for anything in the world, so I'll be hopping on a plane from Paris to L.A. *tout de suite*! If all runs smoothly, I'll be in the Valley to see my baby at five.

Save a big kiss for your dad. We'll go out and show that town how to celebrate birthdays—if I can get my creaky old bones to ignore the jet lag. I'll bring you a special surprise from Paris.

Love and a big bear hug,
Daddy

Kelly's eyes filled with tears of happiness as she read the letter. "Oh, Daddy," she whispered. Suddenly everything was perfect. Kelly rocked back onto the ground with a blissful smile.

First Kirk had asked her out again—proof that he really did like her. And then this incredible, wonderful letter from her father! Kelly couldn't wait to see him and tell him about her plan to stay in Sweet Valley. Then she would have both Kirk and her father!

At seven-fifteen Kelly stepped out of the shower and wrapped herself in a towel. "This bathroom probably qualifies for Federal Disaster Aid," she quipped as she crossed to the sink. "With three people sharing it, we're lucky to get out of here alive."

Jessica rubbed vigorously at a patch of fogged

mirror and met Kelly's eyes in the glass. "The best thing about having tons of money is being able to have a huge bathroom," she declared, outlining her eyes in smoky blue. "You should *see* Lila's—it's humongous. A Jacuzzi, two sinks, mirrors everywhere, lights . . ."

"Sounds like a disco." Kelly giggled. Toweling her hair briskly, she moved into the bedroom. For a long moment she stood contemplating her wardrobe. She wanted to look her best for Kirk. Finally she settled on a pair of white, skin-tight, cropped pants, an oversize red top, and a pair of white sandals.

The phone rang briefly and was cut off as Kelly attempted to pick up Jessica's extension. Shrugging, Kelly went back to blow-drying her hair, letting her mind wander to the magical evening that lay ahead.

There was a gentle knock on the door, and Mrs. Wakefield stepped inside, a serious look on her face. "Kelly—it's your mother on the phone again."

Kelly felt her cheeks flood with color as she met her aunt's gaze. She turned off the blow dryer.

"I really think you should talk to her, dear," said Mrs. Wakefield.

Kelly hesitated for a moment. Now that she had made up her mind to live with her father, she didn't want to think about the fact that she had a mother, too. She felt a sting of resentment toward her mother for interrupting the start of a perfect evening. But the reproachful look in her aunt's eyes made her wince inside. She dropped her eyes and nodded.

As Kelly picked up the phone, Mrs. Wakefield breathed a tiny sigh of relief and let herself out.

"Hi, Mom."

"Hi, Kelly. How are you? Are you having a good time?"

"Uh-huh."

Her mother paused, as though waiting for something more, but Kelly didn't offer to elaborate.

"Well—and how are you getting along in the new school? Is the work about the same?"

Twisting her mouth into a grimace, Kelly sat on the edge of the bed and pulled the phone into her lap. "Yes," she said airily.

"Kelly! I wish—" Mrs. Bates cut herself off as her voice rose in pitch. She started again in a gentler tone. "Kelly, I just want to know you're all right. And I was thinking—"

Oh great, here it comes.

"How would it be if Tony and I came to Sweet Valley next weekend and took you out for your birthday?"

"Sorry, Mom. Dad's coming on Friday, so I'll be with him."

"Oh—of course, sweetheart. I should have known."

In spite of herself, Kelly heard the twinge of disappointment in her mother's voice. "Well, I haven't seen him—" she began.

"No—no, I understand, really," Mrs. Bates insisted. "Have a good time with your father, sweetheart. I love you."

"OK, Mom. 'Bye."

Kelly's hand lingered on the phone as she hung up, and she stared blankly at the crumpled sheets on the bed. But then she caught sight of the clock. It was 7:40. Kirk would be there in twenty minutes. With a surge of anticipation she jumped to her feet to finish drying her hair.

Elizabeth and Jeffrey, curled up on the couch, were watching a movie on the VCR. Kelly fidgeted in her chair and stared distractedly at the screen.

"Did Kirk say he was going to be late?" Elizabeth asked with concern.

"No—no, he didn't call. But I'm sure he just got tied up in traffic," Kelly said, picking at the hem of her red top. She flashed Elizabeth a brief, confident smile and turned her gaze back to the movie.

After ten more minutes, Kelly met another doubtful, questioning glance from her cousin.

"Kelly, you shouldn't let him do this. I think it's pretty rude."

"I *know* there's a perfectly good explanation."

Jeffrey shifted on the couch and gave Kelly a friendly look. "You can come to the disco with us if you want. We're going after this is over."

Kelly shook her head. "Thanks—but Kirk'll be here any minute. He's only—" She glanced at her watch and felt her stomach tighten with anxiety. Forcing herself to sound unconcerned, she continued, "He's only half an hour late. I'm sure it's not his fault."

Just then the door bell rang. "There he is!" Kelly cried. She sprang up from her chair and raced to the front hall. Breathless, she opened the door.

"Don't say anything!" Kirk commanded, holding up his hands in surrender. "I know I'm late and I'm really, really sorry." He gave her a heart-wrenching, boyish smile. "Can you believe I ran out of gas? I was in such a hurry to get here, I didn't even notice the gauge was on empty. Dumb, huh? But I couldn't wait to see you."

Kelly felt her doubts melt away. "It's OK," she assured him with a smile. "No problem."

"Then shall we?" he teased, holding out his arm.

67

Kelly called goodbye to Elizabeth and Jeffrey. Then taking Kirk's arm, she laughed as he escorted her to his white Trans Am and helped her in.

As they drove out toward the coastal highway, they listened to the radio, and Kelly watched Kirk's profile in the lights of the oncoming cars. Every now and then he turned his head and caught her looking at him and smiling happily. But he seemed to think it was perfectly natural, since he just smiled in return.

"Here it is," he announced. They pulled into the parking lot.

Kelly looked through the windshield, past the rows of parked cars. Perched above the dunes, the Beach Disco was a blaze of lights, and the bass beat of the dance music reached them even in the car. In the distance she could see a pale line where the surf met the beach.

"Come on, Kelly. We've got some partying to do."

Inside, the disco pulsed with music and flashing lights, and a huge crowd bobbed and swayed to the rhythm. Kelly held tightly to Kirk's hand as he led her through the crowd, nodding and waving to people they passed. Faces appeared and disappeared, and Kelly thought she recognized some of them from school.

After a few dances, Kirk suggested they go outside. Making their way through the crowd

again, they finally emerged onto the deck behind the disco just as a slow song began. With
a sleepy smile, Kirk drew her into his arms.

"Pretty romantic, huh?" he murmured into
her hair. He tightened his arms around her.
"Soft music, the ocean, the stars . . ."

Kelly shivered with delight and snuggled
closer. She felt as if she were dreaming. "Mmm.
It is." Closing her eyes, she let herself be
swept away.

When the music stopped, Kirk stood back
and asked, "Want something to drink?"

Nodding, Kelly leaned her elbows on the rail
and gazed out at the Pacific. "Sure. Thanks."
She gave him a sidelong glance and smiled. She
couldn't understand why her cousins were so
shocked that she wanted to go out with him. So
far he had been the perfect date—romantic, caring, and flattering. Perfect in every way.

She nodded again. "Thanks, Kirk."

"Hey, no problem. Oh—" He paused, looking across the sand to their right.

"What?"

Frowning, he traced one finger along the railing. "There's an old friend of mine over there.
Would you mind if I . . . ?" His voice trailed off
delicately, his eyebrows raised.

"No—go ahead. I don't mind."

Shaking his head in disbelief, he looked into
her eyes. "You're really great. Most girls would

make a federal case out of it. But she's just an old friend, nothing else."

"I understand, really!" Kelly laughed, giving him a playful shove. "I'll be here."

After a moment of hesitation, he gave her a wave and vaulted over the railing to the sand.

Kelly leaned over the railing, the salty ocean breeze ruffling her hair, and remembered every minute she had spent with Kirk. The more she thought about him, the more she liked him. He was even honest enough to admit he wanted to talk to an old friend without making a big deal about it. She took a deep breath and smiled. Yes, he was special, she decided happily.

After several minutes, though, Kelly began to feel a twinge of impatience. She craned her neck to see down the beach and drummed her fingers on the railing. Catching up with an old friend was fine, but Kelly was starting to feel that Kirk should pay more attention to his *new* friend—her.

Restraining a sigh, she sat down in a deck chair and crossed her legs. She was also beginning to wish he had gotten her that drink, and debated with herself about going off in search of something on her own. Just then, Kirk hurried toward her.

"Sorry," he said quickly as he pulled a chair next to her. "She started in with this real hard-luck story, and I couldn't get back here as quickly as I wanted to. All I kept thinking about was how much I wished it were you I was talking to instead of her. I'm really sorry you had to stay here alone for so long."

Kelly's irritation vanished instantly as she gazed into his intense blue eyes. "That's OK," she replied, "I understand."

"I knew you would." He held out his hand and gave her another one of his irresistible sexy smiles. "Now, how about another dance?" he suggested, pulling her to her feet.

As though hypnotized, Kelly nodded and allowed him to lead her back to the dance floor.

Seven

Elizabeth suppressed a grin and curled her legs up under her on the lounge chair as she watched her twin struggle to put on a brown leotard over her bikini.

"There. Now we put the tails on, and ears, and that's basically it," Jessica explained as she twirled around. "Except for the blindfold or earmuffs or whatever. Hey, where is Kelly, anyway?"

"Here I am." Draping a beach towel over her shoulder, Kelly closed the sliding glass door and joined them on the patio. She sank gracefully into another chaise and looked at Jessica. "This is it?"

"You don't sound very convinced," Elizabeth said with a grin. "Don't you think she looks like a monkey?"

"I can't decide if I should answer that," Kelly replied mischievously. "Either way, it could be dangerous."

Jessica planted her hands on her hips and tipped her head to one side. "Come on, really. We have to wear tights, too—and bare feet."

"*Bear* feet? I thought we were going as the no-evil monkeys."

Elizabeth reached down to grab a towel and threw it over Kelly's head. "Troublemaker."

Giggling, Kelly removed the towel from her head. "Sorry."

Prince Albert, alerted by their clowning around, came padding into their midst, his tail wagging eagerly. It was obvious he was ready to join in the fun, whatever it was.

"OK, Albert," Jessica said, tossing a tennis ball into the pool. They laughed as the dog leapt into the water and swam toward the ball.

"OK, now, listen," Jessica said. Elizabeth and Kelly immediately made solemn faces. Jessica smirked. "*As* I was saying, bare, *naked* feet, the way monkeys have, and *round* ears."

"Like Curious George," Kelly offered, leaning back and crossing her legs.

"Right. Otherwise, we might look like kittens or mice or something."

"You know," Elizabeth said thoughtfully, "the ears go on the *side* of the head on monkeys, not on the top like cats."

"Mmm." Kelly nodded agreement.

Prince Albert scrabbled his way out of the swimming pool and dropped the dripping ball with a triumphant grin. Then he shook himself all over, sending out arcs of spray.

"This party is going to be fantastic," Jessica said happily, dropping into a chair. "People are going to go wild when they see us."

"Yeah, that's why you wanted to wear a leotard," Elizabeth teased. She tossed the ball back into the water. "You just want to show off that gorgeous body of yours."

Jessica arched her eyebrows. "How clever of you, big sister. Seriously, though, everyone knows we're going as the same thing. But they don't know *what* we're dressing as. Lila has tried every sneaky trick in the book to get me to tell her."

"If she offers money, go ahead and tell her," Kelly suggested, her eyes twinkling.

Thinking about the costume party reminded Elizabeth about Nicholas—and Kirk. She turned to her cousin. "Did you call Nicholas yet?"

"Oh—well . . ." Averting her eyes from Elizabeth's gaze, Kelly stammered, "Well, no—not yet. I can't bring myself to do it. He was so nice and everything."

Exasperated, Elizabeth looked away. "Well, are you going with him or with Kirk?"

"I told Kirk last night I'd definitely go with him," Kelly admitted.

"You know," Jessica began, sounding preoccupied as she peeled off the leotard, "I don't get it. I heard from Cara last night that Kirk is going out with Marci Kaplan again."

Elizabeth's stomach clenched, and she looked at Kelly. That sounded like Kirk Anderson.

But Kelly shook her head emphatically. "No—they're just good friends. He told me last night."

"Oh, then I guess Cara was wrong," Jessica decided with a shrug. She tossed the leotard aside and made some minor adjustments to her bikini.

As Elizabeth looked at Kelly, she thought she saw signs of anxiety and confusion. Suddenly her impatience vanished. Poor Kelly was in a difficult position, after all. She had only been in Sweet Valley for a little while, and her life was in a jumbled emotional state anyway. It had to be difficult to keep a level head when there were so many things to think about.

"Hey, let's figure out who's going to be which monkey," she said, changing the subject and easing the tension. With a speculative look at her twin she added, "I guess we can't expect you to be Speak-No-Evil."

"Are you kidding? *Me* with my mouth shut all night? I'd die!" Jessica exclaimed. "No, you should be Speak-No-Evil, Liz. You never say anything bad about anybody."

Elizabeth snorted, thinking of Kirk. "That's what *you* think."

"You know what I wonder," Kelly said doubtfully. "Will anybody be able to figure out what we are?"

"Well, at least we aren't going as the Brontë sisters," scoffed Jessica, sending Elizabeth an impish grin. "*That* was a really good idea you came up with."

"Jessica!" Elizabeth smiled ruefully. "OK, I admit it wasn't the best idea I ever had."

Jessica flipped open a pair of tortoiseshell sunglasses and slid them on. "It's getting to be about that time, folks," she announced. "Show time."

"What? Oh, right—the beach party." Standing, Elizabeth looked expectantly at Kelly. A big group was planning a picnic at the beach that day, and they were all going. "Ready?"

Instantly Kelly glanced at her watch. "Kirk said last night he'd pick me up," she began slowly. "But he said he'd be here twenty minutes ago."

The words set Elizabeth's teeth on edge. She had overheard his glib doorstep excuse the night before, and in her opinion it hadn't been very convincing—even Jeffrey had been skeptical. And now Kirk was late again without calling to let Kelly know.

"Come with us," Elizabeth said impulsively, reaching for her cousin's hand. "You shouldn't have to miss any of the fun just because Kirk can't get his act together on time. Mom can tell him when he gets here, and he'll just meet you at the beach. How about it?"

"Well . . ." Kelly bit her lip, obviously debating with herself what she should do. Jessica tapped her foot and pulled at a shoulder strap.

"OK," Kelly decided with an uncertain smile. "I guess he won't mind."

But you *should*, Elizabeth wanted to say. Instead, she pulled Kelly by the hand toward the kitchen door and flashed a brilliant smile. "Then let's hit the beach."

Kelly stretched forward to rub suntan oil on her shins and let out a blissful sigh. It was a perfect Saturday for the beach: hot and clear, with a brisk, tangy breeze stirring up the waves; perfect in every way—except for the fact that Kirk hadn't shown up yet.

Shouts of triumph broke into her reverie. A game of Frisbee football was in progress, and Jeffrey's team had just scored. Aaron Dallas and Ken Matthews whooped and yelled like Indians, jeering at their opponents.

Nearby, Susan Stewart, Cara Walker, and Maria Santelli were watching the game. "Way to go, Roger!" Maria called out. Roger Patman saluted, then dived into the sand as the Frisbee whizzed by his head. The girls erupted into laughter.

With a faint smile Kelly turned over on her stomach and stared moodily at the surf. *I should have waited for Kirk*, she scolded herself silently. *I shouldn't have come without him*.

Kelly decided to call home and ask her aunt if Kirk had come by for her yet. It was over an hour since he should have picked her up. She scrambled to her feet and looked toward the parking lot. There was a pay phone there. Pausing just long enough to grab some change, she started trudging through the sand to make the call.

But halfway to the parking lot she stopped in her tracks. Kirk was walking toward her with a willowy, dark-haired girl by his side. Their heads were bent close together, as though they were absorbed in a deeply personal conversation.

Suddenly Kelly felt horribly exposed, standing there in her bathing suit, alone.

"Kelly!" As soon as he caught sight of her, Kirk jogged toward her, leaving the other girl behind. Kelly stood perfectly still as he approached.

"Hey, listen, I'm really sorry about this. Marci called me this morning practically having a fit," he explained, taking Kelly's arm and leading her back to the crowd on the beach. Kelly looked over her shoulder at Marci for a second and said nothing.

"You see," he went on easily, "her folks are splitting up, and they're both making her feel guilty. She really needed a friend."

Silently Kelly nodded and sneaked a glance at Kirk's handsome face. She wanted to believe he was telling the truth.

"For any other reason—*believe* me—I would have said no," he added, his voice solemn. "But I hate to turn my back on a friend. I just can't do it."

Kelly nodded again, her heart full. "That's really nice of you," she said, staring at the sand. She felt guilty for having doubted him.

He stopped and faced her squarely. "Believe me, there's nothing going on between her and me."

"I do believe you."

Kirk smiled and ran one finger up Kelly's arm, sending a shiver up her spine. "Great. I knew you'd understand. And you know what? I bet you two would really get along, too."

Some part of Kelly rebelled at the idea. Maybe they would get along, but she didn't see why she should be so understanding of an old girlfriend of his. She gave him a noncommittal shrug.

"Well, anyway, you do understand, that's what counts. You're so much more honest and real than everyone else around here," he continued. "That's how I think of you—as a totally *real* person."

Kirk's words sent a thrill of pleasure through Kelly, and the expression in his eyes as he looked at her intensified it. She was both flattered and excited. With a breathless laugh she broke eye contact with him. "Thanks," she whispered. "I guess I try to be."

He slipped one arm across her shoulders and led her to a clear patch of sand. "Let's set up camp here. Why don't you go get your stuff, and I'll go tell Marci that I'm busy today. I can't let her constantly drag me off to cry on my shoulder." He gave Kelly a significant look.

She smiled in response to his obvious meaning. "OK. I'll be right back."

He tossed her a brilliant grin over his shoulder as he started walking away. "Great—I'll catch up with you in a minute."

A shadow fell across Elizabeth's book. Raising her eyes, she found Kelly smiling down at her.

"Hi, Liz."

"Hey—pull up a towel," she invited with a grin. "What's up?"

"Not much," Kelly replied as she dropped down beside Elizabeth. She drew a few lines in the sand and added casually, "When are you going home?"

Elizabeth pulled her watch out of her beach bag and studied it for a moment. It was almost four-thirty. "Pretty soon, I guess. Why?" She looked at her cousin's averted face and felt a spark of suspicion. "Do you need a ride?"

"Actually, I do—Kirk had to take Marci home. She's really in bad shape."

Elizabeth stared at Kelly in disbelief. "Marci Kaplan? The girl he was going out with?"

"Yeah. Her parents are giving her a really hard time, and Kirk thought she needed a friend," Kelly explained. With a tiny smile she added, "I think it was pretty sweet of him to be so worried about her."

Elizabeth swallowed hard. She didn't know *what* to say. Finally she cleared her throat. "Kelly, are you sure you want to keep going out with this guy?"

"Sure? Of course I am—I really like him a lot. I mean, I'm not exactly thrilled about him taking Marci home, but there's nothing going on with them—they're just friends."

Just friends, Elizabeth echoed in her mind.

She stared down at the water, where Jeffrey was standing knee-deep in the surf, talking to Aaron's girlfriend, Heather Sanford. Jeffrey and Heather qualified as "just friends." But Elizabeth couldn't help thinking that it probably wasn't true with Kirk and Marci. With Kirk Anderson any devious behavior was possible. And as she looked back at her cousin's open, trusting face, she felt afraid for her.

Eight

The sound of muffled whispering and giggling reached Kelly's ears, and she looked up from her book. At the front of the room, Ms. Dalton lifted a finger to her lips while she stared at a pair of girls in the back of the study hall. Sneaking a quick glance at Kirk across the aisle, Kelly ducked her head into *Tess of the d'Urbervilles* again.

It was Thursday, and she and Kirk had been sitting together in study hall all week—since they'd discovered they were in the same study hall. But Kelly had figured out pretty quickly that she couldn't get much studying done with Kirk sitting right next to her. She was much too aware of his presence to concentrate on her work.

She smiled as she peeked at him again through her lashes. Nonchalant and aloof, he sat back in his chair, his long legs stretched out under his desk and his chemistry notes propped up in front of him on a stack of books. A shock of hair had fallen forward across his forehead, and a preoccupied frown gave his profile a stern, almost fierce look.

As though feeling her steady gaze, he looked up at her, a smile lifting the side of his mouth. She blushed and lowered her eyes.

Please don't let it be true about him, she prayed silently, frowning at her open book. *I like him too much already.* All week she had been hearing wisps of rumor floating around—a word here, a broken sentence there. Some of the girls she overheard were positive that he *was* dating Marci Kaplan again. Kelly kept denying it to herself, but she felt a little nagging doubt. She had finally called Nicholas and broken her date with him—all for Kirk. She had to be sure she had done the right thing.

With a brief look up the aisle toward Ms. Dalton, Kelly pulled a slip of paper out of her notebook and scribbled on it hastily: "Are you sure you and Marci are just friends?"

Folding it into a thick square, she tossed it onto Kirk's desk. He looked up in surprise and grinned while he opened it up. His eyes narrowed as he read it.

"Of course we are," he hissed, scowling at her. "I told you that."

"Kirk—quiet, please," Ms. Dalton called out softly.

He directed his scowl toward the front of the room and then grabbed a pen. With a dashing scrawl he wrote on the paper and handed it back to Kelly. "There's nothing going on, so stop worrying about it," his message read.

Kelly's cheeks warmed again. She didn't want to keep prodding, but she couldn't help it. She had to know for sure. Picking up her pencil again, she wrote: "People are saying you two *are* going out. Why would anybody say it if it isn't true?"

Sighing impatiently, Kirk took the note from her and read it while she looked at him with hopeful eyes.

"I don't know why," he retorted in a low, irritated voice. "You shouldn't listen to rumors."

"Kirk? No talking, please."

Kirk frowned and pulled out a fresh sheet of paper from his notebook. Kelly watched his hand anxiously while he wrote: "Kelly, you're the only girl in my life—honest. I asked you to the costume party, right? Marci and I used to go out, but it's all in the past. You're the only one now. Period."

Relief and happiness flooded through her as she read his words. If he said it wasn't true, then it wasn't. She smiled tenderly at him and shrugged. "Sorry," she mouthed.

He shrugged, too, as if to say it didn't matter. With a forgiving grin, he leaned back in his seat again and turned his attention to his chemistry notes. Kelly went back to her own book.

When the bell rang, Kirk pulled his books into a pile and lunged up from his seat. "Hey— catch you later, Kelly. I have to go."

Before she could do anything more than smile in confusion, he was out the door ahead of everyone else. Kelly picked up her books and joined the shuffling crowd as it edged through the door.

As she made her way down the hall, people called out to her or nodded hello or smiled. Already she was part of Sweet Valley High. A warm feeling washed over her, and she hugged her books happily. She wanted to stay in this big exciting school. Her article, "A Stranger's View of Sweet Valley High," had been in Monday's *Oracle*, alongside Elizabeth's preview of the costume party. It had been a hit, but she didn't want to be a stranger any longer, she thought as she pushed open the door of the girls' room. When her father arrived the next day, she would definitely tell him they should stay in Sweet Valley and make it their home. And she was sure he'd say yes.

"Hi, Kelly." Cara Walker was standing in front of a mirror, brushing her glossy, dark brown hair.

"Hi. What's up?" Kelly asked with a smile as she joined Cara by the sink. She leaned close to the mirror and peered intently at her face.

Cara shrugged. "Nothing much," she muttered dryly. She squared her shoulders and smiled at her reflection. Then she turned and leaned against a sink, facing Kelly. "You're going to the costume party this weekend, right?"

"Uh-huh. I can't wait. It'll be my first party in Sweet Valley."

"I heard you and Jess and Liz are all dressing up together. What are you going as?"

Kelly chuckled and pointed a finger at Cara. "Jess warned me about you. It's a secret, Cara Walker. You'll know on Saturday night and not one second before!"

"Can't you even give me a hint?"

"Nope!"

"Ugggh!" Cara tossed back her hair and grinned. "So, do you have a date, or what?"

"Yeah—I'm going with Kirk. I mean, I'm *going* with Liz and Jess, but he's my date."

Cara's eyes widened. "Kirk Anderson?"

Surprised, Kelly raised her eyebrows and started to comb her hair. "Yeah, Kirk Anderson. Why?"

"Well, he has sort of—a reputation. I've heard he's pretty daring, if you know what I mean."

Kelly pursed her lips and tugged at a snarl with her comb. This was news to her. So far, Kirk had behaved like a perfect gentleman. In fact, she had been wondering whether he would kiss her pretty soon. He looked like the type of boy who definitely knew how to kiss, that was for sure. But he hadn't made any moves at all yet.

Kelly decided that Kirk's "reputation" was just another example of malicious gossip. Just like people claiming he was dating Marci and saying he was mean and insensitive when he was very sensitive and caring. Kelly probably knew him better than anyone else, she decided. So she just smiled cheerfully at Cara.

"Well, I'm not worried about him," she said.

Cara tilted her head to one side. "OK, Kelly. I'm just passing on what I've heard."

Kelly laughed and dropped her comb back into her bag. "Thanks for the warning, but I don't think I really need it. See you later, Cara."

In the shower of the girls' locker room, a chorus of laughing soprano voices sang Ernie's "Rubber Duckie" song from "Sesame Street." A metallic clanging of locker doors acted as percussion. Someone shrieked as a wet towel snapped.

Elizabeth was oblivious of what was going on around her. Absentmindedly she fastened her gold lavaliere around her throat.

"Hey, what's wrong, Liz?"

Startled, she looked around. Enid's warm green eyes were fixed on her expectantly.

"Sorry. I guess I'm a little bit out of it." Elizabeth chuckled ruefully. But the smile faded from her lips as her thoughts drifted back to Kelly.

All week Kelly had been in a rising fever of anticipation over seeing her father. Elizabeth couldn't exactly say she was getting tired of Kelly's enthusiastic praise of Greg Bates—that would be mean. But she couldn't help feeling that there was something wrong about it all.

And on top of that, Kelly kept insisting to the twins that she wasn't going back to Tucson. Whenever Elizabeth remembered Kelly's stunning announcement at the Dairi Burger the week before, her stomach turned over. From what she knew of Greg Bates, Elizabeth couldn't understand how Kelly could want to live with her father instead of her mother. But she didn't think there was anything she could do.

"Want to talk about it?" Enid prodded.

"Oh, I don't know." Elizabeth sighed and sat down on a bench. "This whole thing with Kelly and her parents is just so bizarre. I mean—sure, it's great that she loves her father, but she seems to think he's perfect, that he never did a single thing wrong in his whole life."

Enid frowned thoughtfully. "Maybe she just accepts all his problems and loves him anyway."

"No—no, that's not it either. I honestly don't think she knows he even has any faults. And

89

on top of that," Elizabeth went on, "Kelly *completely* blames my Aunt Laura for their divorce—like it was just Aunt Laura who didn't make the marriage work. She seems to think her dad is completely innocent."

"Well, why don't you just talk it all out with her?" Enid asked. "It always makes things worse if they get covered up."

Elizabeth shook her head emphatically. "That's just the problem, though. We're not supposed to say *anything* negative about Uncle Greg. Aunt Laura doesn't believe in prejudicing Kelly against him—"

"So she just lets Kelly believe he's Mr. Nice Guy, right?" Enid finished for her.

"Right." Elizabeth rubbed her jaw, thinking over the situation. "It's really frustrating, Enid."

Cocking her head to one side, Enid gave Elizabeth a doubtful look. "Well, was he really that bad? I mean, these things sometimes get blown out of proportion. Maybe it was just a case of two people being incompatible."

"No—he did some awful things, Enid. Mom says he used to lose his temper all the time and"—she paused and looked sadly at Enid—"he had affairs with other women, too."

"Oh! That is pretty low!"

She nodded. "But he always made all sorts of apologies and excuses—"

There was a pause while Elizabeth stared vacantly into space.

"Liz?"

Swallowing hard, Elizabeth brought one hand up to her throat and fingered her gold chain. She realized that she could have been describing Kirk Anderson with exactly the same words. Did that mean Kelly was falling into the same kind of dead-end relationship Aunt Laura had had? Was Kelly attracted to the same kind of untrustworthy guy? Confused, she shook her head. It was too complex for her to understand.

"Liz?" Enid repeated, looking concerned.

"Sorry, I forgot what I was saying."

"Well, anyway," Enid said, "I don't blame your aunt for wanting a divorce." She pursed her lips in disgust. "There's no excuse for that kind of sneaking around."

Elizabeth nodded. Standing up, she grabbed her book bag, and she and Enid headed out of the locker room. She had to admit that her aunt *had* made excuses for a long time. But something more must have happened that tipped the scales, something that Aunt Laura couldn't bring herself to excuse at all.

With a muffled sob Kelly jerked awake. She lay in bed shaking, one hand pressed to her mouth.

"Kelly?" Jessica's voice was thick with sleep. "Did you say something?"

Kelly turned her face away. "I—I just had a really bad cramp in my leg," she lied, squeezing her eyes shut.

"Oh. Mmm." The other bed rustled and creaked softly as Jessica rolled over. Then Jessica raised herself slightly. "You didn't have another nightmare, did you?"

"No—no, it was just a really awful cramp in my calf. It woke me up."

"OK. G'night." With a sleepy murmur Jessica sank back down again.

Kelly waited for Jessica to speak again, but there was nothing but silence. A bar of light from a passing car slid across the ceiling while Kelly counted to ten. Down the street a dog barked. Kelly had no idea what time it was, but she wished the night would end soon.

Finally she let out a long, tired sigh and tried to relax. Already the panic and confusion of the nightmare had melted away as though she had never experienced it at all—the noises, the closed-in feeling, the fear, the sense of being all alone and abandoned.

It was only a dream, she told herself sternly, willing herself to forget it all. *It wasn't real. It was only a dream.*

Nine

"Good morning, Liz."

"Morning, Mom. Hi, Dad." Elizabeth smiled at her parents as she slid into her chair at the breakfast table and reached for a piece of toast. "It's Kelly's birthday today," she reminded them. "I guess we finally get to meet the infamous Uncle Greg."

Mrs. Wakefield made a wry face and began peeling an orange.

"Who knows, Alice?" Mr. Wakefield put in suddenly. "He may have changed for the better since we knew him. Let's wait and see for ourselves."

"Well, I'm sorry!" Mrs. Wakefield exclaimed. "I just can't forget the way he treated my sister. Don't expect me to welcome him with open arms—"

"Hi, everyone!" Kelly bounded into the kitchen, beaming with excitement.

Elizabeth jumped up from her chair to hug her cousin. "Happy birthday!" she cried.

"Happy birthday, dear," Alice Wakefield said.

"Hear, hear," added Ned Wakefield.

Wrinkling her nose, Kelly sat down at her place and propped her chin up in her hands. "You know how you always expect to feel older on your birthday? I never do. I feel the same as always."

"You don't start feeling older on your birthday until you're thirty," Mrs. Wakefield said with a chuckle. "Then each one gets more and more painful."

"Well, then you don't have to start worrying about that for a few more years, do you, Alice?" Mr. Wakefield asked with exaggerated innocence. She rapped him lightly on the head with a rolled-up section of newspaper but gave him a loving smile.

"Hi, everyone," said Jessica as she slouched into the kitchen with a huge yawn. She scratched her head sleepily. "What's for— Oh, happy birthday, Kelly!"

Grinning from ear to ear, Kelly clasped her hands together. "I just can't believe Daddy'll be here today. I can't wait to see him."

Elizabeth smiled, but she couldn't help taking a quick peek at her mother. Mrs. Wakefield looked as if a struggle were taking place within her. Finally she drew a deep breath and smiled.

"Kelly, we thought we'd have a little predinner birthday party for you when he gets here. That way we can all help you celebrate, and then you and your father can go out somewhere special by yourselves."

"Oh, you don't have to do that!"

"We want to, Kelly." Elizabeth put one hand on her cousin's arm and gave her a reassuring squeeze. "Everyone deserves the VIP treatment on her birthday."

Kelly looked at each of them in turn, her eyes shining. "Thanks a lot, you guys. It's so sweet of you all. And I know Daddy'll really think so, too."

"We're doing it for *you*," Mrs. Wakefield put in hastily. She stood up and carried her dishes to the sink. "Ned and I will both get home early, so when your father gets here at five, we can have a little party for you."

Kelly's eagerness was visible to everyone, and Elizabeth couldn't help feeling a pang of alarm. She glanced at her mother, and they exchanged a worried look before Mrs. Wakefield lowered her eyes and shook her head slightly. Elizabeth prayed that everything would work out as perfectly as Kelly expected it to. But she couldn't help wondering if it was even possible.

"How does this look, Jess?" Elizabeth asked.

She arranged the last sesame cracker in an artistic fan around a wheel of Brie and held up the cheeseboard for her twin's inspection.

"Perfect. Put a little parsley on the Brie, and it'll be ready for *Gourmet* magazine."

Giving her sister a lopsided grin, Elizabeth crossed to the sink, where a little pot of parsley sat on the sunny windowsill. She snipped off a sprig and placed it with exaggerated care in the center of the cheese. "*Voilà*."

Jessica giggled and picked up a tray of glasses and the pitcher of iced tea. She cast a quick glance at the kitchen clock. "Hey, Liz—it's five o'clock, and Dad isn't home yet."

"Don't worry. I'm sure he'll be home soon." Elizabeth lifted the cheeseboard and followed her twin into the living room.

Kelly, dressed in a new skirt and blouse, paced back and forth across the room. She gave the twins a bright, nervous smile as they came in. Mrs. Wakefield sat alone on the couch, her hands folded in her lap as she watched Kelly pace. On the table was a small stack of wrapped presents, and Elizabeth shifted them to make room.

"He should be here any minute now," Kelly said. She pushed a lock of hair behind one ear and smoothed her skirt with trembling hands.

The sound of a car door slamming reached their ears, and Kelly flew to the front door. The twins and Mrs. Wakefield maintained an apprehensive silence.

"Sorry, just me," came Mr. Wakefield's voice from the front steps.

He appeared in the doorway of the living room, briefcase in hand. "Sorry I'm late," he told his family as he loosened his tie. "I had a last-minute crisis."

Elizabeth saw a significant look pass between her parents. She knew exactly what their word-less communication was: Where was Kelly's father?

"So, what's going on in school these days?" Mr. Wakefield asked casually, sitting down on the couch.

Jessica looked at Elizabeth and Kelly and then at her father. "Are you talking to me, Dad?"

"Sure."

She looked confused and pursed her lips in concentration. "Nothing, I guess."

Sitting on the arm of the couch, Elizabeth crumbled a cracker to bits in one hand. They were all trying to pretend it was just a typical evening, but there was a definite feeling of ten-sion in the air. Kelly wasn't even bothering to follow the conversation. She kept pulling the curtain aside and peering anxiously out into the street.

Mrs. Wakefield cleared her throat. "Who'd like some iced tea? Kelly?"

"What? Oh—" Kelly frowned at the coffee table, as though she couldn't quite figure out what the question had been. "I guess so. I know Dad'll be here in a minute. He probably got tied up in traffic from L.A."

"I bet you're right," Mr. Wakefield said quickly, nodding his head for emphasis.

Kelly looked imploringly at Elizabeth. Blushing, Elizabeth nodded. "Yeah—you know, I read an article in the paper about how rush-hour traffic has gotten to a real crisis level."

Across the room Jessica met her gaze with a skeptical grimace. Swallowing hard, Elizabeth brushed the crumbs in her hand into a napkin and balled it up fiercely. One glance at her watch told her Kelly's father was now twenty minutes late. So far, Greg Bates was running true to his reputation.

"Why don't you open your presents, Kelly," Jessica suggested. She flung herself into a chair and hooked one leg up over the arm. "Try to guess what Liz and I got you."

Kelly shook her head. "No—I'd rather wait for my father, if that's OK."

Jessica shrugged.

"So . . ." Mr. Wakefield let out a long sigh and looked at his wife for cues. Mrs. Wakefield was staring fixedly at her hands in her lap. "So, anyway . . ." he began again without getting anywhere.

Suddenly Mrs. Wakefield stood up. "I'm going to start making dinner," she announced. She paused for a moment. Kelly was still looking out the window, and Mrs. Wakefield looked at Kelly's back without speaking. Then, clenching her jaw, she turned and hurried into the kitchen.

Minutes passed with agonizing slowness. With an apologetic smile in Kelly's direction, Mr. Wakefield switched on the six o'clock news, and Elizabeth and Jessica drifted over to join him. Out in the kitchen their mother rattled pots and pans—venting her frustration, Elizabeth suspected glumly. Kelly continued her vigil at the window, coming up with new suggestions every now and then for why her father could be so late.

At six-thirty Prince Albert let out a bark, and Kelly leaped to her feet. "He's here!"

Elizabeth was gripped with nervousness. Finally she was going to see for herself what kind of a person Kelly's father was.

"Daddy!"

"Hi, princess. How's my baby?"

In the living room everyone rose hesitantly to their feet and exchanged awkward looks. Mrs. Wakefield hurried in from the kitchen, wiping her hands on a towel and glaring at the door.

"Well, hello, everyone. You cannot believe the traffic. I only wish I had a car phone so I could have called. This is one date I hate to be late for."

Greg Bates strode confidently into the room

with one arm across his daughter's shoulders, a disarmingly candid smile on his face.

Elizabeth felt herself staring and quickly glanced at Jessica, who was suffering from the same shock. In spite of seeing his picture, she hadn't expected him to be so good-looking. In person Greg Bates was magnetic and charismatic. It was obvious in the way he smiled and in the sparkle in his eyes. At once Elizabeth could see why Kelly was so crazy about him.

"Alice! You look fantastic!" he exclaimed, enveloping Mrs. Wakefield in a hug she couldn't avoid. "And, Ned—good to see you. How've you been?"

Kelly stood beside him, her eyes shining with love. All traces of her agonizingly long wait had vanished from her face, leaving nothing but adoration and joy.

"Here are Liz and Jess, Daddy. I bet you wouldn't have recognized them, would you?"

He turned on the twins with an inquisitive arch to his eyebrows. Smiling slightly, he looked at Jessica and then at Elizabeth. "Let me think—you're Liz, right?"

"That's right!" Elizabeth gasped, smiling in spite of herself. "How did you know?"

"That's my secret," he teased.

Jessica grinned with delight and met Elizabeth's surprised look.

"Please sit down, Greg," Mrs. Wakefield said formally.

He gave her a penetrating look and then sat with easy grace.

"So, how was your flight from Paris, Dad?"

"Smooth as silk," he said, smiling as he leaned back in his chair.

Just then the door bell rang. Mr. Wakefield rose to answer it. He returned with a huge floral arrangement in his arms. "Delivery for Miss Kelly Bates!"

Kelly jumped up. "Daddy! They're so beautiful! I can't believe it. This is so incredibly gorgeous!" Quickly she took the card out of the arrangement.

Impressed, Elizabeth admired the huge bouquet. There were dozens of flowers of all kinds: roses, carnations, lilies, freesias, snapdragons, and feathery ferns. She watched with an expectant smile as Kelly wrestled the tiny pink card from its envelope.

"Oh. They're from Mom." Kelly's voice was flat and toneless as she read the note. " 'Happy birthday, Kelly, with all my love, Mom.' " With a little shrug she pushed the card back into the bouquet and turned away.

"Listen, Kelly, I want to explain why I didn't bring you a present," her father said, his face solemn.

"You don't have to—" Kelly began.

He held up one hand. "No, your birthday comes only once a year. I did find the most beautiful antique writing desk in Paris, and it was perfect for you. But the shipping would have taken at least three months, and I couldn't let you wait that long."

Elizabeth frowned, puzzled. Kelly's father didn't want to make her wait for her birthday present, so he brought nothing? That didn't make any sense.

"Oh, Daddy. I don't care if you get me something or not. I'm just so happy you're back," Kelly insisted.

"That's my girl," he said fondly.

"And you know, I was thinking," she continued, glancing quickly at Elizabeth for support. "Maybe you could move back to Sweet Valley, and I could live with you instead of Mom."

There was a tiny gasp of surprise from Mrs. Wakefield, and Elizabeth looked at her mother nervously. Alice Wakefield's face was drained of color.

"Well, sweetheart, that's a terrific idea!" Greg Bates slapped his palms on the arms of his chair for emphasis and gave Kelly a nod. "That's one terrific idea, and we can talk about it when I get some things settled."

"When will that be?" she asked eagerly.

"Soon, honey. Soon. But for now"—he took one look at his watch and said mournfully—"I'm sorry, but I have to get back to L.A.—a late business dinner, sweetheart."

Kelly looked stunned. "But, Dad—" she began, her voice as small as a child's.

"I know, honey. I hate to do this to you, but I can't miss it. I'll call you real soon, and we'll talk about that idea of yours, OK?" With a dazzling smile, he pushed himself to his feet and took Kelly's hands. "How about a smile for your dad?"

Looking as if she might start crying, Kelly nodded and managed a quavering smile.

"There's my girl! Now give me a big kiss, and I've got to run. It was great seeing all of you again. You look fantastic," he added, giving the family a jaunty wave as he headed for the door. "I'll see you all soon."

Kelly followed him to the door.

A painful silence filled the room the moment they had gone. Shocked, Elizabeth stared at her sister, slowly shaking her head. Jessica stared back, wide-eyed.

"I'll *never* forgive him for this," Mrs. Wakefield whispered, her voice filled with tears. She struggled to her feet and ran to the kitchen.

103

Ten

Kelly shut the door softly and leaned against it for a moment after her father had driven off. His parting words, "Sorry, princess. I'll call you soon," echoed in her ears. A tear trembled on her lashes, then rolled down her cheek, and she brushed it away absently.

It was so unfair that the traffic had been so bad and had made him late—and she hated the person he had to have a stupid business dinner with. But at least she had seen him after all this time. That was something. Taking a deep breath, she squared her shoulders and lifted her chin.

When she went back into the living room, her aunt and uncle were both gone. The twins were sitting stiffly on the couch, looking strangely embarrassed. Kelly couldn't understand what was wrong.

"Well, what did you think of him?" Kelly prompted with an eager smile as she sat down on the edge of a chair. "Isn't he wonderful?"

"He's—pretty funny," Jessica admitted slowly.

"Yeah, isn't he?" Kelly agreed. She looked at Elizabeth. "Didn't you like him, too?"

"Oh, well—I guess so," Elizabeth stammered, not meeting Kelly's eyes. "It's too bad he had to leave and—and everything."

Kelly pressed her lips together to keep them from trembling as the disappointment came flooding back. "Yeah, he was so sorry about it, too. That dumb guy he has to have dinner with couldn't make it any other time." She plucked at the hem of her skirt.

Jessica let out a little snort of disgust. "Well, I would be *so* furious if that happened to me. I mean, it's your *birthday*."

"It's not his fault, though!" Kelly cried. "He couldn't help it if the traffic was really bad— and if that guy couldn't have a meeting with him any other time. It's not his fault," she insisted stubbornly.

"Well, whoever's fault it is, it's still a complete disappointment for you."

"Kelly," Elizabeth put in quickly, giving her twin a swift warning look, "why don't you open your present from us? We picked it out specially for you, since you'll be spending so much time at the beach."

With a halfhearted shrug Kelly nodded and knelt down in front of the coffee table. "Which one is it—the red one?"

105

Elizabeth nodded.

"Go ahead," Jessica urged, moving forward to the edge of the couch. Her eyes sparkled with anticipation. "I want to see if you like it."

"OK." Trying her best to look enthusiastic, Kelly ripped the paper off the bulky box. Inside was a huge red- and white-striped beach towel with a matching striped canvas beach bag. "These are really nice," she murmured, spreading them out flat on the floor.

She stared down at them for a moment and thought she might start to cry. Forcing a bright, quavering smile, she looked up again. "Thanks a lot, you guys. I mean it."

"Happy birthday," Elizabeth said with a sympathetic smile. "We can all go out later and do something really great, how's that?"

Kelly nodded silently. If things had worked out, she would be having a wonderful, special dinner with her father right now. Her heart ached with missing him and wishing he didn't have to leave so quickly. It was so unfair.

"You did like my dad, didn't you?" she repeated, needing to be reassured. It was important to her that her cousins like him as much as she did and that they see what a wonderful, terrific father he was.

Elizabeth and Jessica exchanged glances, and Elizabeth cleared her throat. "Well, he—he, uh, reminds me a little of Kirk."

Something in her tone caught Kelly's ear, and she lifted her chin defiantly. "What do you mean?" she demanded.

"Oh, just—I don't know," Elizabeth said. She looked away. "I don't know what I meant."

An awkward, strained silence separated Kelly from her cousins. She sat slumped on the floor by her new beach towel and bag, feeling lost and alone. There had definitely been a critical note in Elizabeth's voice, and whether she was criticizing Kirk, or Kelly's father, Kelly was hurt and upset by it.

Jessica squirmed around on the couch into a new position and punched a pillow into shape. She sighed loudly. "So . . . those flowers are really nice. Aunt Laura must have spent a fortune on them."

Kelly swiveled around to look at them, as if for the first time. Tears welled up in her eyes. Everything had started with her mother's unreasonable decision to leave her father—it all stemmed from that one terrible mistake.

"It's all her fault!" she choked out, wiping her eyes furiously. "It's all Mom's fault this ever happened!"

"Kelly!" Elizabeth gasped, shaking her head in disbelief. "She isn't even *here*! How can you say that?"

"I don't care. It *is* Mom's fault! She's ruined everything I ever wanted to do and—and I hate her!"

107

Elizabeth and Jessica stared at her in shock. With a strangled cry of despair, Kelly pulled herself to her feet and ran sobbing out of the room.

Kelly jumped when she heard a car door slam out in the driveway, and she turned back to her book again. She had been staring vacantly at the swimming pool for the last few minutes. *Stop moping*, she scolded herself sternly. *Things will work out just fine.*

She felt a rush of shame as she recalled her childish outburst after her father had left the previous evening. She knew her cousins were stunned by her display of anger. And, she admitted grudgingly, it wasn't her mother's fault that her birthday had turned out to be such a complete and utter disaster. But still . . .

The patio door slid open smoothly, and Jessica and Elizabeth came outside, laden with packages.

"The moment of truth!" Jessica sang out cheerfully. "We have exactly five hours to whip these costumes into shape."

An armload of paper bags tumbled out of Elizabeth's grip onto the picnic table. Sighing tiredly, she sank into a lounge chair and flopped backward. "I am wiped out. Never—*never* shop with my sister," she warned Kelly solemnly.

"The Spanish Inquisition could have used it as a torture."

"Ha-ha. What a comedian," Jessica shot back as she upended a brown paper bag. Plastic-wrapped packages of tights slithered into a heap.

Kelly smiled tentatively and joined them at the picnic table. She wasn't sure how her cousins would react to her after the way she'd behaved the night before. But they seemed to have forgotten—or forgiven—the scene. They acted as though nothing at all had happened.

"We got five pairs of black tights," Jessica explained, ripping open one package. "Three we cut the feet off of for us, and the others we cut up for tails."

Kelly's eyes twinkled as she opened a package and unfurled the tights. "Are you sure this is going to work?" she asked.

"Skeptic," Elizabeth scoffed.

"Come on, let's get started here. I'll go get the scissors," Jessica continued. Kelly and Elizabeth exchanged a knowing grin. Jessica loved to be the commander in chief.

"Just tell me what to do, O Great One," Kelly intoned reverently, putting her palms together. Jessica stuck out her tongue, and Kelly giggled. Maybe things weren't so bad after all, she thought hopefully. In just a few hours they would make their debut at the country club costume party, and they were sure to be a big hit. And afterward, she and Kirk would go some-where romantic. . . .

After Jessica had turned and raced back into the house, Elizabeth heaved herself up out of her lounge chair and picked through the bags on the table. She gave Kelly a soft smile.

"You're a pretty OK person," Elizabeth said lightly.

A rush of warmth spread through Kelly, and she smiled in return. "You're pretty OK your-self. I—I'm sorry about what I said—you know."

Elizabeth shook her head. "Listen, I know how upset you were last night. Let's just forget it."

Nodding with relief and gratitude, Kelly opened another bag and extracted three long-sleeved black leotards. It was hard to believe she had only been living with her cousins for two weeks. She felt closer to them every day. She sent Elizabeth another broad smile and turned her attention back to the costumes.

"We should have white stomachs," she mused as she held one of the leotards up against her body. "Don't you think?"

"Mmm. Good idea. We can cut ovals of white iron-on interfacing. I know Mom has a whole bunch of it."

"OK, I'm back," Jessica announced. She was dragging a stuffed pillowcase.

"Jessica, what is that?" Elizabeth asked with an incredulous laugh.

"Socks. All of mine, yours, and Dad's." With a casual flick of her wrist, Jessica dumped a huge mound of socks out onto the patio. They rolled off in all directions.

Kelly eyed the pile skeptically and retrieved two pairs from under the table. "I probably shouldn't ask this, but what are the socks *for*?"

"Our tails. I've figured out how to do them. Watch." Frowning with concentration, Jessica snipped the legs off one pair of black tights and proceeded to stuff one leg with socks. Kelly and Elizabeth watched in anticipation.

"There. How's that?" Jessica held up the sock-stuffed tail to her rear end and looked over her shoulder at them with a hopeful expression.

A muffled giggle erupted from Elizabeth, and she shook her head apologetically. "Sorry, Jess. But to tell you the truth, it looks like a sausage—all lumpy."

Jessica's face fell. She whipped the tail around to examine it.

"It's the foot," Kelly decided after a moment's study. "It's shaped. Cut it off right over the heel and tie it off."

"*Very* clever," Jessica agreed. She bit her lip in concentration as she popped out the socks and cut off the foot. Then she tied the leg, turned it inside out, and restuffed it.

"Perfect!" crowed Elizabeth. "It's really perfect."

Kelly took the tail and waved it around experimentally. "Wait—I have an idea. If we take some wire, like a hanger, and twist it in like a curlicue, wouldn't that make it look even more like a monkey's tail?"

The twins exchanged glances. "Brilliant," Elizabeth declared.

"I'll be right back." Jessica dashed once more to the patio door.

Elizabeth hitched herself up on the table and smiled. "Jessica really gets into this kind of thing."

"I can see that!" Kelly laughed and twirled the tail around some more.

Moments later Jessica returned with three wire coat hangers. Without a word she handed one to each of them, and they all busily twisted them open and straightened out the kinks.

"Now . . ." Jessica snaked her hanger wire into the sock-stuffed stocking and then wrapped the tail into a flat coil. She held it up to the base of her spine. "Well? Yes?"

"Yes, definitely," Kelly said.

"It really looks like a monkey tail now," Elizabeth said. "You couldn't confuse it with anything else. It'll be obvious what we are."

"That's good. Everyone has been bugging me to tell them what our costumes are," Jessica said breezily. "They'll just die when we walk into the country club. People will just—"

"Go ape?" Elizabeth supplied, raising her eyebrows.

112

Kelly grinned. "This is going to be more fun than a barrel of monkeys."

"Enough! Quit with the monkey jokes," Jessica groaned.

"OK. Sorry." Kelly tried to keep a straight face, but when she caught Elizabeth's eye, they both burst into giggles again.

"And now for the pièce de résistance," Jessica went on, ignoring them. She fished around in another bag. "We found these at a gag store." She pulled out three pairs of huge flesh-colored plastic ears fixed onto wire headbands.

"Jessica!" Kelly jumped to her feet and held out her hand eagerly. "These are fantastic!" She slipped one pair on her head and looked at her cousins. "How do I look?"

Jessica screeched with laughter. "They're a riot," she cried, putting on her pair. She stuck her tongue into her lower lip and swung her arms by her sides, doing a perfect imitation of a monkey.

Laughing hysterically, Elizabeth and Kelly mimicked Jessica, bouncing and loping around the patio and climbing up on the table. Then doubling over with giggles, Kelly dropped down on the grass and held her side.

"It looks like the natives are getting restless," came a voice from the patio door.

Kelly looked up hastily, swallowing a last giggle, and her face flushed pink. "Steven!"

She whipped the fake ears off her head the moment she remembered they were there.

Steven Wakefield, the twins' older brother, was leaning against the doorframe with his arms folded across his chest, a big grin on his face. "Hi, Kelly. How are you?"

"Fine! I'm—" She broke off as she scrambled to her feet. She knew her face was scarlet. But as she met Jessica's dancing eyes, she started laughing again. "Hi, Steve," she said, crossing the patio to give him a big hug.

He shook his head. "Somehow this scene doesn't surprise me." Then he laughed and tousled Kelly's hair. "How've you been? I'm sorry it's taken me so long to get home to see you. I've been up in Puget Sound doing research for a term project."

"That's OK. If you had come before, you might have missed this as your first glimpse of me in all these years."

Steven laughed. "Well, I sure wouldn't have wanted to miss this. What's going on, anyway?"

"We're all going to a costume party," Jessica said as she flung herself into a chair. "We're going as See-No-Evil, Hear-No-Evil, and Speak-No-Evil."

Steven looked at his sisters and then at Kelly. He slowly shook his head. "Dad'll have to take a picture of this for posterity."

"Good idea," Elizabeth put in. "We'll be ready

114

to go at eight o'clock. You'll see us all decked out as monkeys—the works."

"I can't wait." Then he snapped his fingers. "Hey, Jess, I almost forgot. I copied down some numbers of professors who need baby-sitters, like you asked."

Jessica took the crumpled piece of paper Steven fished from his pocket and ran her eyes down the list. Earlier she had informed Kelly that her friendly rivalry with Lila Fowler created a constant demand for cash, and a constant demand for new sources of income.

"OK, thanks," she muttered, tucking it into her pants' pocket. Then she gave her brother a grin and moved away from him, hopping up and down, monkey-style, and scratching under her armpits.

"If this is the effect you have on my sisters, Kelly, I'm not sure you should stay too long," Steven said mock seriously. "They're wild enough already."

Suppressing a grin, Kelly shook her head. She planned to stay in Sweet Valley forever.

Eleven

"Jessica, stop smirking," Mr. Wakefield ordered. He squinted into the camera again and rotated the lens for a moment.

"I can't help it, Dad. I get like this on Saturday nights." Jessica fidgeted with her ears and shot her mother an impudent grin. Mrs. Wakefield chuckled.

Elizabeth shifted her weight and felt her tail swinging behind her, dragging on her leotard. It poked Kelly in the leg.

"Hey!"

"Oops! Sorry."

Jessica made a face at the camera. "Dad, hurry up! This is taking *forever*."

"All right, all right. I'm just checking the focus. OK, girls. Say 'bananas'!"

"Bananas!" they cried in unison as Mr. Wakefield snapped the picture.

116

Kelly looked at her watch. "Shouldn't we get going? It's getting late."

"Jessica likes to make her entrances," Mrs. Wakefield commented with an amused smile. "She prefers to be about fifteen minutes late."

"Oh, Mom!"

Elizabeth smoothed the white patch on her stomach and straightened her sleeves. Now that they were fully dressed in their monkey costumes, she was brimming with excitement. Hard as it was for her to believe, they really did look like monkeys with their bare feet and big ears and their hair pinned up out of the way. She gave her twin and her cousin a smile. "This is going to be great. Let's go."

"Girls, I think whichever of you is driving should wear shoes," Mrs. Wakefield pointed out calmly. She raised her eyebrows a fraction when none of them volunteered. "Girls?"

"OK, Mom." Jessica sighed. "Liz, you drive."

"Me?" Elizabeth looked at her sister and then shrugged. "Fine. I'll take them off in the parking lot. We'd better take our tails off for now, too. You guys hold onto them and we can attach them when we get to the dance." She took off her tail and handed it to Kelly.

"Great. Now let's go!"

Laughing and chattering, the three girls got into the Fiat. Elizabeth started the engine and pulled away. It was still light enough for people to be outside on their lawns and on the side-walks, and whenever someone caught a glimpse of the three monkeys riding in a red convertible, his or her mouth dropped open in astonishment.

With a huge grin Elizabeth pulled out onto the highway. In minutes they were turning up the broad, sweeping drive of the Sweet Valley Country Club, and Elizabeth swung into a space. The parking lot was already crowded.

"OK, tails and bandannas, everyone," Jessica commanded as they scrambled out.

Elizabeth kicked off her shoes and put on her tail. Then she tied a red bandanna across her mouth. She was Speak-No-Evil. Jessica and Kelly put on their tails, and then Jessica tied her scarf over her huge ears, and Kelly blindfolded herself.

"I'll have to hold on to one of you," Kelly muttered as she tied the knot behind her head.

"Don't worry, I'll protect you." Elizabeth laughed, her voice muffled and distorted through the gag.

Jessica frowned. "What did you say?" Impatiently she edged the bandanna away from her ears. "This is never going to work. I can't hear a single thing. And my interfacing is starting to peel off. And my tail keeps poking me. Let's go before we totally fall apart."

Linking arms, the three girls headed for the brilliantly lit main building of the country club.

As they climbed the steps, they heard the opening chords of "Dance Bop," one of The Droids' popular original songs. Elizabeth pushed open the door, and the three monkeys stepped inside.

"Jess, Liz—Kelly! What—what are you?" Lila Fowler ran up to them immediately, a puzzled frown on her face. She was wearing a short blond wig with a tiara, a strapless blue evening gown, and huge swags of rhinestones around her neck.

"What are *you*?" Jessica's eyes were wide as she took in her friend's costume.

"Princess Diana."

Elizabeth suppressed a snort of laughter. More of their friends started to gather around, trying to figure out what their costumes were.

Enid, dressed as a hippie, folded her arms. "Well, monkeys, I guess."

"That's right," Elizabeth agreed, grinning impishly as she lifted one side of her gag. "What kind of monkeys?" Her eyes landed on a boy dressed as a ragged, dirty wino, and her mouth dropped open. "Jeffrey?"

He kissed his hand to her. "Ev'nin', m'dear," he slurred, and swayed drunkenly to one side. He gave her a wink from completely sober eyes.

"Well, I'm trying to figure this out," Lila continued, her hands on her hips.

"I wish you guys would hurry up so I can take this blindfold off," Kelly piped up in a

119

voice of exaggerated patience. "I feel like I'm missing the party."

"Blindfold, gag—" Enid snapped her fingers and pointed at them triumphantly. "See-No-Evil, Speak-No-Evil, and Hear-No-Evil, right?"

"Hey, that's right!" Lila crowed. "That is perfect!"

The crowd that had gathered around them started to break up, and Elizabeth pulled her bandanna off. With a sigh of relief, Kelly took off her blindfold and grinned happily at Elizabeth before looking around.

"This is great," she said, chuckling and taking everything in. "Hey, who is that in the Donald Duck outfit?"

"It's Ken," Susan Stewart replied, sweeping her thick red hair back over her shoulders. She was wearing a 1940s-style sun dress, and her hair was curled and parted far to one side. She was dressed as a movie queen from the golden age of Hollywood.

"You look just like Rita Hayworth," Elizabeth decided after studying her for a moment.

Susan laughed. "That's exactly right! No one else knew who I was trying to be."

As Susan drifted away, Enid moved to Elizabeth's side. She wore a braided leather headband across her forehead, love beads around her neck, and her tie-dyed shirt was covered with peace signs and buttons.

"Whose idea was it to come as the monkeys?" she asked, batting at Elizabeth's curly tail.

"I don't remember, really. It just sort of evolved." Elizabeth hitched up one shoulder of her leotard and looked over to where Kelly had begun dancing with Kirk Anderson. It suddenly occurred to her how ironic it was that Kelly had been See-No-Evil: Kelly couldn't see what was going on right in front of her own eyes.

"Well, Kelly sure is appropriate," Enid observed dryly, voicing Elizabeth's thoughts.

Elizabeth sighed. "I know." She watched her cousin gazing up into Kirk's handsome face. "At least Marci Kaplan isn't here tonight—that's something, anyway."

"Hmm."

"Attention, everyone!" Dana Larson, lead singer of The Droids, tapped her microphone. The popular high school band was dressed in army fatigues. "Attention! We're going to have the judging early, since a lot of the costumes don't look like they'll stand up to serious dancing. And we *are* going to *dance!*"

A loud whoop and thunderous applause reverberated through the big ballroom.

"OK," Dana continued. "The judges have been circulating, and we have a few winners already." She read from a card in her hand.

"First, for most authentic costume, Sandra Bacon. Step forward, Sandy."

There was a round of applause as Sandra gave a low curtsy. She was dressed in an intricately embroidered Mexican dress, with a black lace mantilla over her head and shoulders. Her eyes lingered on her boyfriend, Manuel Lopez, as she took her bows.

"That's really nice," Elizabeth whispered to Enid. Out of prejudice, Sandy's parents had at first resisted the idea of her dating a Mexican-American boy, but they had come to respect and like him.

"And for most creative, Winston Egbert! Way to go, Win!" Dana laughed as Winston, the junior class clown, walked to the front of the room to a huge round of applause.

Daring as ever, Winston had come as a bunch of grapes. He had dozens of purple balloons stuck to him, and a collar of huge felt grape leaves around his neck. He grinned as his balloons bobbed and swayed while he walked.

"Look out you don't get popped, Win!" Ken Matthews called out from the crowd.

Winston narrowed his eyes menacingly. "Anybody who touches my balloons is dead meat."

"We'll have some more finalists later," Dana continued. She pulled the microphone off its stand. "But right now we've got some music to play! One, two, one-two-three—"

As the band burst into a dance tune, Jeffrey stumbled up to Elizabeth and leered at her. "How 'bout a dance, bee-yootiful?"

She giggled. "I don't even want to touch you. You're disgusting."

"I am not," he retorted, looking offended. With great dignity he smoothed his impossibly wrinkled baggy jacket and rubbed at the soot on his cheeks. "I am a perfect gen'lmun."

Even in dirty rags and broken shoes Jeffrey looked great to Elizabeth. She hooked her tail up over one arm and gave a little curtsy. "I guess I'll be brave and take a chance."

There was a loud pop across the room. Jeffrey raised his eyebrows. "I think Winston might be under attack," he said, chuckling, as another explosion sounded.

"Oh, no! I hope he's wearing something under his grapes!"

With a laugh Jeffrey took her by the hand, and they let the music move them across the dance floor.

On the other side of the room, Jessica slipped through the door to find the ladies' room. As she turned the corner, she ran into a girl in a wet suit and snorkeling mask coming the other way.

"Oooph—sorry," Jessica gasped, making a wild grab for her ears as they slipped.

The girl pried off her face mask and breathed

a sigh of relief. It was Robin Wilson, Jessica's co-captain on the cheerleading squad. "Hi, Jessica," she said. "Great costume."

"Thanks. Hey, listen—" Jessica paused for a moment, looking at the other girl's face. Robin was staring blankly at the mask in her hands, but she looked up with a guilty start when the silence became noticeable.

"Sorry. What?"

"I just thought we should try to get together tomorrow afternoon—about the new routines and stuff and the new schedule."

"Sure—sure. That's fine."

With a slow nod, Jessica stepped aside to let Robin pass. "OK—I'll stop by around three."

Robin nodded mechanically but didn't move. She cleared her throat. "That's fine," she repeated.

Jessica glanced over her shoulder as she pushed open the ladies' room door. Robin still hadn't moved yet. *What's wrong with her?* Jessica wondered to herself. Then she put Robin out of her mind and hurried to the mirror to check her makeup.

"Did I tell you how great you look?"

Kelly smiled up into Kirk's face as their bodies swayed in time to the music. "Yes—about five times."

And so do you, she wanted to add. She couldn't get over how sexy and gorgeous Kirk looked dressed as a pirate. With a black patch over one eye, a leather vest worn open over his bare, muscular chest, and a very real-looking dagger stuck in his belt, he looked swashbuckling and devilish.

A shiver of excitement rippled through her as she read the admiring gleam in his eye. She knew that before the night was over, she would be in his arms somewhere, kissing him.

"How about a drink? Are you thirsty?"

"Mmm. I guess so."

He gave her a challenging look. "Some of this Kool-Aid they're pushing here or something stronger? I've got some beer in the car."

"Some of the Kool-Aid, I guess," she replied with a smile. "I don't really like beer."

"Really," Kirk said, looking disappointed. "Well, you don't mind if I—?"

"No, it's OK."

He pulled her a little closer. "Don't worry—I can handle a few beers, no problem."

"I'm not worried," she murmured into his shoulder. "I trust you."

"Mmm. Good."

Kelly snuggled into Kirk's arms and closed her eyes.

"Listen, how about you and me having a private party of our own?" he whispered, his voice husky and low and caressing. "Just you and me."

"That sounds like a great idea," she whispered back.

He pulled away and looked into her eyes for a long moment. "Then what are we hanging around here for? Let's go."

Taking her hand, he led the way through the crowd of dancing couples. All around them were Indians and clowns, Raggedy Ann dolls and cowboys. It was like being in a dream, Kelly thought, a magical fantasy world set to music. She paused for a moment in the doorway and made a last quick survey of the room. It had been fun, but it was time to be alone with Kirk. Smiling, she met his eyes and let him pull her out the door.

Twelve

Kirk and Kelly were silent as they strolled out to the parking lot, listening to the music fade behind them. Kirk draped one arm casually across her shoulders. He smiled at her in the faint light of the floodlamps.

"Here," he murmured, opening the passenger door of his white Trans Am and helping her fit her curling tail in. He leaned through the open window. "There's a place called Miller's Point we can go. It's got a great view."

"A great view, huh?" she teased softly, meeting his eyes with a faint smile. Jessica had told her all about Miller's Point: it was Sweet Valley High's premier make-out spot. "Sure. I'd love to see the view."

He grinned knowingly and came around to the other side of the car to get in. A six-pack of beer clinked at his feet as he started the car.

"Want to share a beer with me?"

"No, thanks."

Kirk shrugged and twisted off a cap. The car surged forward along the highway and began climbing the hill to Miller's Point.

With a blissful sigh, Kelly leaned back against her seat and closed her eyes, letting the warm ocean breeze blow on her face from the open window. It was a perfect night—fun, romantic, and full of promise.

"Hey, you know, I never wished you a happy birthday," Kirk said when he stopped the car.

She shook her head, hypnotized by his dark eyes as he leaned toward her. "No, you didn't."

"Happy birthday, then."

Kelly closed her eyes as his lips met hers, and a shiver of excitement ran through her. He was as good a kisser as she had expected.

Finally he pulled away. "I brought a blanket," he whispered hoarsely. "Let's sit outside where there's more room." He picked up the six-pack carrier, slipped his half-empty beer bottle into it, and reached into the back for a blanket. Then, with a lingering smile, he pushed open his door and climbed out.

Kelly helped him spread out the blanket on a patch of grass and then sat down with her knees tucked up to her chin, staring at the valley stretched out below. "So many lights," she said, sighing happily. "They're like stars."

"Mmm." Kirk leaned toward her and kissed her neck. "You look so sexy in that leotard," he murmured, running one hand up her arm. The warmth of his touch seemed to go right up her arm and down the other side. "You're just about driving me out of my mind."

"Is that right?" she replied lightly. She sighed dreamily. "It's so beautiful up here."

Kirk nodded and took a long pull on his beer. "So are you."

Flattered, she turned to look at him, her lips parted. Before she could speak, he leaned forward and kissed her again, this time more urgently. One hand caressed her shoulder and began edging under her leotard.

"Mmm—Kirk, no." She took his hand away from her shoulder and pulled away, then looked searchingly at him.

"You're not afraid, are you? A big girl like you?" His voice was teasing, cajoling, but a little hard, too. The beer bottles clinked again as he shifted his legs on the blanket.

"I just like to take things a little slower, that's all."

He kissed her again. "Slow, huh? I like living fast, Kelly. I thought you knew that."

Kelly had to fight against the thrill of his kisses—he was almost too good to resist. But she needed to make it clear that kissing was all she was prepared to do. His hand traveled insistently up her arm again, and she shrugged it off, feeling uneasy.

"Kirk—really. I mean it."

"Now, wait a second. I've taken you out a few times, and I think it's about time for you to start showing some appreciation."

"*What*?" Kelly suddenly felt a chill of fear.

"You heard me." Kirk swallowed the last of his beer and gave her a long look. "It's time to grow up, Kelly. Or are you just a tease?"

She gasped. "A *tease*? I never—"

His mouth came down on hers again, cutting her off in midsentence. He wrapped his arms tightly around her and pressed her to him. With growing panic she tried to struggle free. "Kirk! Cut it out! I mean it!"

Breathing harshly, he stared at her in the darkness, anger evident on his face.

"I—I think maybe you should take me home," she stammered, close to tears. She scrambled to her feet.

"Kelly—hey, wait a second." Cursing loudly, Kirk sprang up and grabbed her arm.

Without thinking she kicked him hard in the shin, and he cursed again angrily. She stood there in shock, trying to control her racing heart.

He gave her a venomous look and stepped back a pace, kicking the six-pack. Whirling around, he picked up an empty bottle and hurled it furiously into the darkness. It hit a rock out-

130

cropping a few yards away and exploded. The shattering sound burst through the darkness.

Kelly froze. That sound—the sound of breaking glass sent a ripple of fear running through her. "Don't—don't do that," she whispered, her throat dry.

With a hard, malicious laugh, Kirk flung another bottle at the rocks. It shattered instantly.

"Please! Don't!" Kelly was breathing heavily, backing up step by step and shaking her head. "Please, don't!" Her hands went to her ears, trying to shut out the noise.

"I'll do anything I want to, dammit," Kirk yelled. "So live with it!" Taking careful aim, he threw another bottle against the rocks. The smashing of glass filled the air.

A choking sob welled up in Kelly's throat, and she turned blindly, desperate to get away. There was something horribly familiar about the scene: the crashing, the darkness, the swearing and shouting. And the same unreasoning, overwhelming panic that always paralyzed her in her nightmare was back—stronger than ever. She had to get away. Crying, she began running back down the road, stumbling and tripping.

"Kelly! Come back here!"

A car door slammed, and the Trans Am's powerful engine roared into life. Tires squealed as Kirk spun the car around and came racing down the hill after Kelly. The car braked next to her.

"Get in. I'll take you home," Kirk said impatiently through the open window. "Come on, get in!" His voice rose to an angry shout.

"No! No, get away from me!" she screamed. Hysterical, Kelly turned to keep running. There was something horrible she was trying to get away from, something more than just Kirk.

The car idled loudly for a moment, and then Kirk pulled away, sending up a spurt of gravel as he raced down the road. Stranded and alone, Kelly sank to her knees, sobbing in the weeds by the side of the road as the last piece of the puzzle fell into place in her mind.

It was the sound of breaking glass that haunted her dreams, and thundering, out-of-control anger. The scene swam dizzily into focus at last, and she remembered it all. She was eight years old, hiding under the kitchen table, her hands over her ears, while her father raged with the fury of a hurricane at her mother. She heard dishes smashing to the floor. It was a methodical, piece-by-piece destruction of every plate and bowl and glass in the cupboards.

Her mother was pleading, begging her father to stop, and grabbing his arms. Cursing, he threw her off, and when he wouldn't stop destroying everything he could, she fell sobbing next to Kelly and ordered her to run next door for the neighbors. But Kelly couldn't move. She was frozen in place as she watched her father storm out of control.

"Daddy! Don't do it!" she cried, pressing her hands to her face. "Daddy! No! Stop it! Mommy!"

Devastated, Kelly cried and cried now as though her heart were breaking. She couldn't stop. Small rocks and sticks pressed into her legs as she knelt in a crumpled heap on the road to Miller's Point. Now that she could remember what her nightmare was, she also came to a horrible realization. The dam in her mind had finally broken. That horrible nightmare scene had been real.

Thirteen

Jeffrey stopped his car in front of the Wake-fields' house and cut the engine. He and Elizabeth sat in comfortable silence for a moment, listening to the crickets and the breeze stirring the leaves.

Elizabeth yawned and stretched luxuriously. "Ohhh . . . that was a good dance, wasn't it?" Smiling, she rubbed her head where her monkey ears had pinched a little too hard.

"Mmm . . . Dana really sounded great—the whole band did."

Elizabeth nodded, her thoughts on the costume party; Winston trying to keep everyone from popping his balloons, Lila pretending to make Aaron Dallas a peer of the British Empire, The Droids introducing their newest song with a big fanfare, Jessica twirling her tail like a burlesque dancer . . .

Elizabeth let her gaze linger on the darkened house. No one was home yet. "Want to come in?" she asked Jeffrey. "We can watch TV and have some ice cream."

"What flavor?"

She let out a short chuckle. "Does that make a difference?"

"Of course it does," Jeffrey replied, his eyes sparkling mischievously.

"I think I can dig up some double chocolate royal," Elizabeth replied dryly. Shaking her head, she opened the door and grinned at Jeffrey. "Come on, you bum."

As she put the key in the front door, another car pulled up behind Jeffrey's. They both turned, curious.

"That looks like Tom McKay's car," Elizabeth said, surprised.

"Liz!" Jean West, Tom's girlfriend, rolled down the window on the passenger side. Her face was drawn with worry. "God, I'm glad you're home. We picked Kelly up by—"

"What?" Stunned, Elizabeth ran out to the street, Jeffrey right behind her. She peered anxiously into the backseat. "Oh, my goodness. What happened?"

Jean and Tom both climbed out of the car, and Jean pushed her seat forward. "I don't know, Liz, honest. She was crying when we

135

found her, and she couldn't tell us what happened."

Her heart pounding, Elizabeth leaned into the backseat. Her cousin was huddled in the corner, crying softly into her hands. Kelly's hair was a mess, and her tights were snagged and ripped. "Kelly! Kelly, what happened?"

"Oh, Liz," Kelly moaned, shaking her head.

Fighting an urge to start crying herself, Elizabeth pulled her cousin gently by the hands and helped her out of the car.

Jeffrey met her eyes with a look of deep concern and worry. "Do you want me to call your mom and dad?" he asked.

Elizabeth looked down at her cousin, who was leaning against her and crying into her shoulder. A surge of anger and pity coursed through her. She shook her head.

"Maybe you'd better just go home," she said in a low voice. "I'll call you later." She appealed to Jean. "Could you help me get her upstairs?"

"Sure, Liz."

The two of them walked Kelly into the house while the boys stayed outside. Elizabeth maintained a grim, steely silence as she and Jean helped her cousin up the stairs and into Jessica's room. Still crying softly, Kelly sank onto her bed.

Jean looked at Elizabeth with embarrassment.

"Jeez, Liz. I'm sorry—I don't know what to tell you—"

"That's OK, Jeanie. Thank you so much for bringing her home. I really appreciate it. Tell Tom I said thanks, too."

The petite, dark-haired girl nodded quickly. "I guess I should go. Is there something I should do?"

Elizabeth shook her head. "No, thanks, Jean. I'll take care of her."

"All right. I can let myself out."

Elizabeth shut the bedroom door behind Jean and then ran quickly to Kelly's bedside.

"Kelly? Can you tell me what happened?" She shook the girl's shoulders gently. "Try to stop crying and tell me what's wrong. Was it Kirk?"

Kelly shook her head dismally. "No—no—" Still sniffing and choking, she shook her head again.

Elizabeth went into the bathroom and ran cold water over a washcloth. Then she brought it back and wiped Kelly's tear-stained face. With a shuddering gasp, Kelly swallowed hard and tried to straighten up.

"Kelly! Did something bad happen? *Tell* me." Elizabeth heard her voice rising in panic, and she had to force herself to stay calm.

"Yes—but it's not what you think." Kelly took the cool washcloth from Elizabeth and wiped her eyes. Drawing a deep breath, she stared at the floor. "I—Kirk and I had a fight, and he started yelling and stuff, and I remembered—I remembered—" Kelly shuddered once again.

Elizabeth nodded encouragingly and knelt in front of her cousin, taking her hands. "What, Kelly? What did you remember?"

"Why Mom left Daddy."

Stunned, Elizabeth sat back on her heels. She swallowed hard. "What?"

There was a look of despair in Kelly's eyes when she met Elizabeth's gaze. She let her breath out slowly. "Dad totally lost his temper one night and went berserk—he was screaming and yelling and breaking everything in the house," she said in a voice so low, Elizabeth had to strain to hear.

"Mom couldn't get him to stop. She tried to get me to go to the neighbors for help, but I was too scared. Anyway, the neighbors heard the noise and called the police. That's when my mom took me to Tucson. I've been having nightmares about it ever since, but I could never remember them when I woke up." Kelly shook her head, as though trying to clear it.

Elizabeth felt herself staring in utter horror at her cousin. It was too horrible to believe.

"Kelly, are you *sure* you didn't just dream it? I mean, are you positive it really happened?"

Kelly stared at her mutely for a long moment.

Her chin trembling, she cried out, "Liz, how could I *dream* something that bad about my father? I—I *love* him!" Tears spilled down her cheeks again, and she raised clenched fists to her eyes.

"Oh, Kelly." Filled with pity and sadness, Elizabeth sat next to her cousin and wrapped her arms around her. If it was true, it explained a lot. It would explain why Aunt Laura had suddenly packed up and left and never wanted to go back.

Elizabeth sat with her cousin, hugging her close, until Kelly fell into an exhausted sleep. Carefully Elizabeth swung Kelly's legs up onto the bed. She stood looking down at her for a moment. Kelly looked so small and vulnerable and lonely that Elizabeth thought she herself might burst into tears.

Setting her jaw, she turned off the light and went downstairs to wait for her parents.

Elizabeth sat in grim silence in the living room as Jessica and her parents arrived home simultaneously.

"Hi, sweetheart," Mrs. Wakefield called out. She unbuttoned her trench coat as she walked into the living room but stopped when she saw Elizabeth's angry face. "What is it, Liz?"

139

Jessica and Mr. Wakefield came in behind her. "Is something wrong?"

"I have to tell you all something," Elizabeth began in a low, intense voice. The others sat down warily, their faces showing a hint of alarm.

With many starts and stops to regain control of her anger and her tears, Elizabeth told them all what had happened with Kelly. As her daughter spoke Mrs. Wakefield's face registered a sweeping range of emotions, from shock and outrage to pity and anguish and love.

"Is it true, Mom?" Jessica whispered when Elizabeth had fallen silent. "Is that what happened?"

Mrs. Wakefield put one hand over her face and shook her head. "I don't know," she moaned. "I just don't know, Laura never talked about it. I knew Greg had a temper. But I thought she left because she found out he was seeing someone behind her back."

"Well, there's one thing I know." Mr. Wakefield spoke up, his face grim. "Whether she wants to or not, Laura has to tell—if not us, then at least Kelly—*exactly* what happened."

Mrs. Wakefield nodded silently.

"But why did she keep it a secret?" Jessica wailed. "I don't get it."

"I don't know, honey," Mr. Wakefield said in a sad, tired voice. "Maybe she was ashamed—maybe she felt guilty. There could be lots of reasons. People don't usually know why they do things, I'm afraid. But *if* it's true, it must have been very traumatic for your aunt."

"It's true. I'm sure it is." Mrs. Wakefield sniffed, shaking her head. "I always knew Laura wouldn't have left him unless there was something really awful." With a tearful sigh she added, "She really did love him very much."

Elizabeth pressed one hand against her mouth and stared at the floor. She had rarely seen her mother so upset.

"You'd better call Laura," Ned Wakefield said quietly, looking lovingly at his wife. "I think we should get this settled once and for all."

Alice Wakefield nodded and drew a shaky breath. "I'll call her right now," she said firmly as she rose to her feet. "That poor child deserves to know the truth."

Fourteen

Sitting on the patio, Elizabeth couldn't concentrate. Her eyes kept straying from the arts section of the Sunday paper to the windows of the den. Whenever she glanced at her mother, she found her staring anxiously in the same direction.

By the pool, Jessica rolled over onto her stomach and propped her chin up on her fists. She was watching the house, too. "How long are they going to be in there?" she wondered aloud.

Mrs. Wakefield shook her head. "As long as it takes."

Elizabeth looked at her twin and shrugged. There was no telling what was being said inside the house. Their aunt had arrived on the first plane from Tucson that morning, and she and Kelly had been alone together since she got to Sweet Valley. That had been nearly two hours ago.

Suddenly the patio door slid open. Looking strained, but also wearing a faint smile, Laura Bates stepped outside and pushed the door shut behind her.

"Kelly decided she needs a few minutes by herself," she said. She lowered herself wearily into a chair by her sister, and Mrs. Wakefield patted her arm gently.

"I guess I owe you an apology—" Kelly's mother began.

"No, Laura. Don't apologize," Mrs. Wakefield said hastily. She gave her sister a tender smile. "You don't have to apologize to us."

"Well, an explanation, then—please. I want to tell you what happened. What's *been* happening."

Mr. Wakefield nodded. "Anything you feel comfortable telling us, Laura. Whatever you want."

Elizabeth looked intently into her aunt's face. *She looks so much like Mom*, she decided. At the moment she also looked tired and careworn, but relieved, too, Elizabeth thought.

"It's true, what Kelly told Liz last night," Mrs. Bates began. She stared into the pool, as though seeing the scene all over again. "Greg blew up that night—what the reason was, I don't even remember. But it seemed as if he just couldn't stop. He was totally out of control. When he wouldn't stop yelling and breaking

143

things, I was terrified. It was so bad that the neighbors called the police."

Mrs. Wakefield held her sister's hand and nodded sympathetically.

"After the police arrived, he calmed down. But I didn't know if it would happen again or if he would hurt himself or me—or Kelly. I just couldn't take that risk. So I packed her up, and we left and never went back." Her voice caught as she finished, and she swallowed convulsively. "And I never let her come out here to visit him. I was too afraid."

"Why didn't you tell us, Laura? We were so worried about you."

"I know, Alice. I know. But, well, I just couldn't. At first I was in such a state of shock, I couldn't even believe it myself. And then, it seemed so—" She shook her head. "There wouldn't have been any point in dragging it all out in the open."

Elizabeth's heart went out to her aunt. The pain of the experience didn't seem to have lightened at all over the years. But she still couldn't understand why her aunt had let Kelly go on believing Greg Bates was so perfect.

"I know what you're thinking," Laura Bates said with a sigh. "Kelly. Why didn't I tell her her father wasn't what she thought he was?" She paused for a moment and looked down at her hands.

144

"Well," she said at last, "once I realized Kelly had blocked the whole thing out of her mind—that she really didn't have any memory of it—I didn't have the heart to tell her. Greg isn't a bad man. He just can't handle the responsibilities that go along with being a husband and a father. I thought if they only saw each other when he chose to visit, that she would see the best side of him."

Elizabeth looked quickly at her own father and realized once again how lucky she was to have him. He met her look and smiled sadly.

"I've seen a lot of bitter women poison their children against their ex-husbands," Laura Bates went on. "I couldn't do that to Kelly. But I also knew I couldn't be reasonable and levelheaded about it either. If I started criticizing Greg, I never would have been able to stop."

Silence fell over the group on the patio. Right or wrong, Elizabeth realized that what her aunt had done had taken a lot of strength.

Jessica sat up and curled her legs under her. "Aunt Laura, what about Kelly? What's she going to do?"

Their aunt gave the twins a tender smile. "Why don't you both go ask her? I know she has some things she wants to say to you."

Elizabeth met her sister's uncertain look and nodded for both of them. They rose together and went inside.

Upstairs, Jessica rapped gently on her own bedroom door. "Kelly? Can we come in?"

The door swung open, and Kelly faced them with a tremulous smile. A sudden wave of shyness swept over them all for a moment.

"Well . . ." Kelly began.

Elizabeth gave her a doubtful look. "Well?"

"Well, for goodness sake," Jessica huffed, pushing them both into the room. "Let's stop acting like a bunch of strangers."

Kelly laughed suddenly. "Yes, ma'am."

"So—how did things go with your mom?" Elizabeth asked once they were settled on the two beds. "I mean, are you all right?"

"Yeah, I guess so," Kelly admitted, pleating the blanket beneath her fingers. "It was pretty emotional, though."

"I bet," Jessica agreed with a smile.

"Mom told me about—you know—why she left Dad and why she didn't want to tell me about it."

"Do you still want to live with him?" Elizabeth had been wanting to ask that question since the previous night.

Kelly pursed her lips. "Yes and no. I mean, I still love him for all his good qualities, but I guess he just can't handle being a full-time father. I can see now that he isn't exactly perfect."

"So, what are you going to do?" Elizabeth asked.

146

"You could stay here with us," Jessica put in quickly. Her smile was earnest and hopeful and open.

"Thanks—but I think I should go home," Kelly replied. She bit her lip. "I've really been hard on Mom lately. I want to prove I'm not such a crummy kid."

"She doesn't think you're a crummy kid. You know that," Elizabeth chided her gently. "She really loves you."

Kelly nodded. "I know it. Now. I've been a total jerk."

"Well, not *total*," Jessica corrected her.

Elizabeth met Kelly's eyes and a silent message passed between them. Simultaneously they grabbed the pillows and whomped Jessica over the head.

"I give up! OK! OK!" Gasping, Jessica slithered off the bed onto the floor. She peeped up at her cousin and grinned impishly. "And you're not going out with Kirk the Jerk anymore, are you?"

"Well . . ." Kelly looked down at her lap. Then she looked up with a sheepish grin. "He's a *really* good kisser—"

Jessica squealed with disgust and put her hands over her ears. Laughing, Elizabeth hit Kelly with the pillow.

"But he *is* a total jerk, just like you said," Kelly admitted quickly. "So no more See-No-Evil for this girl. Get him *away* from me."

The three girls exchanged a meaningful look and burst into laughter.

Jessica pulled the Fiat up the Wilsons' driveway and turned off the engine. After grabbing her shoulder bag, she hopped out of the convertible and jogged up to the house. The door opened as she reached the front steps.

"Hi, Jessica. Come on in," Robin said.

"Hi." With a brief smile Jessica edged past Robin and into the house. "I got the new schedule of games from the coach," she continued briskly as she settled herself on the sofa and pulled a pen from her bag.

Robin sank into a chair across from her and nodded absently. Her brown eyes were clouded with anxiety, and her face was pale and drawn. She opened her mouth to speak but didn't say anything.

Curious, Jessica lowered her pen and stared at Robin. One of the things about Robin that impressed everyone was her ability to take on a lot of responsibility. She successfully juggled high grades, competitive platform diving, a boyfriend, and cheerleading. But now Robin looked totally dazed.

"Robin?"

Robin jumped slightly in her chair. Blinking rapidly, she licked her lips. "Jessica? I think you should know—I may not be on the squad next year."

Jessica's eyes widened in surprise. "What? Why?"

"Well . . ." Robin lowered her eyes. "See, I applied to college—Sarah Lawrence, in New York—early admission."

"That's when you go a year ahead of time, right?" Jessica prompted. This was the first she had heard of Robin's college plans.

Robin nodded. "Yeah, and—and—"

"*What?*"

The girl's chin quivered uncontrollably. "And I was accepted!" With that, Robin burst into tears and ran out of the room, leaving Jessica stunned and speechless.

Will Robin Wilson's aunt take control of Robin's life, forcing her to leave Sweet Valley and go to college in the East? Find out in Sweet Valley High #46.

Coming next month: the second Sweet Valley High Super Thriller, **ON THE RUN.** *A new boy in town is attracted to Elizabeth. When he won't talk about his past, Jessica and another intern on* **The Sweet Valley News** *decide to find out all about him—and what they learn is more than they've bargained for!*

Get Ready for a Thrilling Time in Sweet Valley®!

☐ **26905 DOUBLE JEOPARDY #1**   **$2.95**

When the twins get part-time jobs on the Sweet Valley newspaper, they're in for some chilling turn of events. The "scoops" Jessica invents to impress a college reporter turn into the real thing when she witnesses an actual crime—but now no one will believe her! The criminal has seen her car, and now he's going after Elizabeth ... the twins have faced danger and adventure before ... but never like this!

**Watch for the second Sweet Valley Thriller
Coming in May**

Prices and availability subject to change without notice.

Buy them at your local bookstore or use this handy coupon for ordering:

SWEET VALLEY HIGH

☐	26741	DOUBLE LOVE #1	$2.75
☐	26621	SECRETS #2	$2.75
☐	26627	PLAYING WITH FIRE #3	$2.75
☐	27493	POWER PLAY #4	$2.95
☐	26742	ALL NIGHT LONG #5	$2.75
☐	26813	DANGEROUS LOVE #6	$2.75
☐	26622	DEAR SISTER #7	$2.75
☐	26744	HEARTBREAKER #8	$2.75
☐	26626	RACING HEARTS #9	$2.75
☐	26620	WRONG KIND OF GIRL #10	$2.75
☐	26824	TOO GOOD TO BE TRUE #11	$2.75
☐	26688	WHEN LOVE DIES #12	$2.75
☐	26619	KIDNAPPED #13	$2.75
☐	26764	DECEPTIONS #14	$2.75
☐	26765	PROMISES #15	$2.75
☐	27431	RAGS TO RICHES #16	$2.95
☐	26883	LOVE LETTERS #17	$2.75
☐	27444	HEAD OVER HEELS #18	$2.95
☐	26823	SHOWDOWN #19	$2.75
☐	26959	CRASH LANDING! #20	$2.75

Prices and availability subject to change without notice.

Buy them at your local bookstore or use this convenient coupon for ordering:

- -

Bantam Books, Dept. SVH, 414 East Golf Road, Des Plaines, IL 60016

Please send me the books I have checked above. I am enclosing $_____ (please add $2.00 to cover postage and handling). Send check or money order —no cash or C.O.D.s please.

Mr/Ms _____

Address_____

City/State _____ Zip _____

SVH—5/88

Please allow four to six weeks for delivery. This offer expires 11/88.

☐	26682	**RUNAWAY #21**	$2.75
☐	26745	**TOO MUCH IN LOVE #22**	$2.75
☐	26689	**SAY GOODBYE #23**	$2.75
☐	27492	**MEMORIES #24**	$2.95
☐	26748	**NOWHERE TO RUN #25**	$2.75
☐	26749	**HOSTAGE! #26**	$2.75
☐	26750	**LOVESTRUCK #27**	$2.75
☐	26825	**ALONE IN THE CROWD #28**	$2.75
☐	25728	**BITTER RIVALS #29**	$2.50
☐	25816	**JEALOUSY LIES #30**	$2.50
☐	27490	**TAKING SIDES #31**	$2.95
☐	26113	**THE NEW JESSICA #32**	$2.75
☐	27491	**STARTING OVER #33**	$2.95
☐	27521	**FORBIDDEN LOVE #34**	$2.95
☐	26341	**OUT OF CONTROL #35**	$2.75
☐	26478	**LAST CHANCE #36**	$2.75
☐	26530	**RUMORS #37**	$2.75
☐	26568	**LEAVING HOME #38**	$2.75
☐	26673	**SECRET ADMIRER #39**	$2.75
☐	26703	**ON THE EDGE #40**	$2.75
☐	26866	**OUTCAST #41**	$2.75
☐	26951	**CAUGHT IN THE MIDDLE #42**	$2.95
☐	27006	**HARD CHOICES #43**	$2.95

Prices and availability subject to change without notice.

Buy them at your local bookstore or use this handy coupon for ordering:

- -

Bantam Books, Dept. SVH2, 414 East Golf Road, Des Plaines, IL 60016

Please send me the books I have checked above. I am enclosing $_____
(please add $2.00 to cover postage and handling). Send check or money order
—no cash or C.O.D.s please.

Mr/Ms _____

Address _____

City/State _____ Zip _____

SVH2—5/88

Please allow four to six weeks for delivery. This offer expires 11/88.

Special Offer
Buy a Bantam Book
for only 50¢.

Now you can order the exciting books you've been wanting to read straight from Bantam's latest catalog of hundreds of titles. *And* this special offer gives you the opportunity to purchase a Bantam book for only 50¢. Here's how:

By ordering any five books at the regular price per order, you can also choose any other single book listed (up to a $5.95 value) for only 50¢. Some restrictions do apply, so for further details send for Bantam's catalog of titles today.

Just send us your name and address and we'll send you Bantam Book's SHOP AT HOME CATALOG!